Louisa knelt and dipped the pot in the stream. The cold water sent goose bumps up her arm and down her back. She shivered, then glanced down. The world receded around her. The chorus of songbirds faded. Lou heard only the pounding of her heart and saw only the tracks that had not been there the evening before; huge misshapen, yet human in outline. She counted four claws, the middle claw longer than the rest. They were suggestive of a bear, but no bear ever made tracks like these.

Suddenly Lou heard the birds and the wind and felt the warmth of the sun on her face. It reminded her that she was alone and unarmed and in the same woods as something that had apparently come down from the glacier to stalk them in the dead of night. Another shiver ran through her, but this one had nothing to do with the cold water.

Lou stood and started to back away from the stream. Too late, she sensed a presence behind her. She started to open her mouth to shout for Zach when her shoulder was gripped and she was spun halfway around.

The *Wilderness* series:

WILDERNESS #52:
GLACIER TERROR

DAVID THOMPSON

LEISURE BOOKS NEW YORK CITY

Dedicated to Judy, Shane, Joshua, and Kyndra.

A LEISURE BOOK®

June 2007

Published by

Dorchester Publishing Co., Inc.
200 Madison Avenue
New York, NY 10016

ISBN-10: 0-8439-5714-X
ISBN-13: 978-0-8439-5714-3

Printed in the United States of America.

Visit us on the web at www.dorchesterpub.com.

WILDERNESS #52:
GLACIER TERROR

Prologue

The animals feared the Thing in the glacier. They feared it the most on the nights of the full moon. For that was when the Thing emerged from the icy depths of its lair.

The deer in the thickets, the squirrels in their treetop nests, the rabbits and badgers in their burrows, heard the piercing howls, and trembled.

Part of their fear was instinct. They were always wary of the unknown, and the Thing in the glacier was unlike anything, anywhere. It was different from them, different from all that was.

Part of their fear was experience. The Thing hunted them and slew them, ate their flesh and drank their blood. Big or small, it made no difference. The Thing even killed bears and mountain lions, creatures that normally preyed on everything else. When the Thing was abroad, the bears and mountain lions slunk off into the shadows and wanted nothing to do with it.

As time passed, the Thing had to roam farther afield to find the succulent flesh it craved.

So it was on a night when the full moon hung golden and huge above the miles-high peaks that the Thing emerged and moved to the edge of the ice cliff. Below and away stretched a mountain and a valley. The Thing threw back its hairy head and voiced its challenge, a cry not like those of any other animal in the valley, more shriek than howl but not really either. It froze deer in their tracks. It caused a roaming black bear to turn and hasten elsewhere. It startled an owl into flight.

With eager tread the Thing descended to the forest below the glacier. It moved as silently as the wind, with a peculiar shuffling gait. Often it stopped to tilt its head to listen and sniff.

The Thing came to a bench sprinkled with boulders. Far down the mountain was the lake the Thing seldom visited. A grunt of surprise escaped the Thing at the sight of pinpoints of light where there had never been lights before. Its brow furrowed, and an ominous growl rumbled deep in its barrel chest. The Thing knew what those lights meant and did not like it.

Then the wind shifted, and an acrid odor brought the Thing's head up to sniff anew. It glanced to the northeast, and there, much nearer than the lake, was another point of light that flickered and danced as if alive.

The Thing snarled. It was displeased. Yet, at the same time, it tingled with expectation, for where there was fire, there were those who made the fire, and those who made the fire were no different to the Thing than deer or mountain sheep or grouse. They, too, were prey.

The Thing glanced at the lake and the other points of light, then turned and made for the nearer one. It moved with consummate care, seeming to be part of the night itself.

Sounds reached the Thing's ears. The sounds made by the creatures that had made the fire. The sounds made no sense to the Thing. They were not growls or snarls but an unending babble that reminded the Thing of the chatter of chipmunks. The Thing bristled, and its long nails clicked and clacked.

Soon, very soon, the Thing would get to do that which it most loved: to rip and rend and tear. The Thing's mouth watered. It craved flesh—raw, ripe flesh—to fill its belly and give it life, and it would not be denied.

There were four of them.

From his place of concealment, the Thing studied the intruders.

They were young. They had oval faces and high cheekbones and long, flared nostrils. Two wore their hair in braids, two wore their hair loose and flowing. All wore garments of deer hide, shirts, and leggings, the leggings decorated with beads. Their shirts had long fringe on the arms.

The four were well armed. Each had a knife. Three had tomahawks. Quivers filled with arrows lay near them, as did the bows that let the arrows fly. One had a spear close to his legs. Another had a war club.

They talked and laughed and gnawed at rabbit meat they had roasted on a spit.

The Thing suppressed a growl. Of all the creatures it encountered in its domain, it disliked these the most. It knew they came from the north, not the south; although how it knew, it could not fathom.

They were unaware they were being watched. One added a branch to the fire, and the flames grew brighter but not so bright that the light reached to where the Thing crouched in the dark.

The tallest of the four turned and pointed at the distant lake and the pinpoints of light and said something that caused the others to stop smiling and laughing.

The Thing was irritated by their chatter. Everything their kind did irritated it. Which was partly why the Thing made a special point of hunting them when they dared venture this close to the glacier. They had not done so in a good long while. But now they were here, and the Thing would do to the four as it had done to all the others. To that end, the Thing slowly unfurled and crept forward.

Suddenly the Thing froze. It had been careless. Beyond the four, hidden in the shadows, were the animals that had brought the four. The animals their kind always rode rather than go about on their own two legs. And one of the creatures had raised its head and whinnied. It had caught the Thing's scent.

The whinny silenced the four at the fire. They rose to their feet, their weapons in hand, and regarded the animal that had warned them. Then they stared in the direction the animal was staring, straight at the Thing.

The Thing did not move, did not twitch, did not voice its annoyance. It knew it must not do anything to spook the four or they would jump on their mounts and race like the wind for the valley floor. As fast as it was, the Thing could not hope to catch them. So it froze and waited, and presently its patience was rewarded. The animal that had whinnied lowered its head, and the four by the fire sat back down and resumed their chatter.

The Thing still did not move. It was too wise, too canny in the ways of the stalk and the kill. It waited, and when the four at long last ceased their babble and lay down to sleep, the Thing crept near the ring of firelight and crouched.

The time had come.

Chapter One

If there was anything more exasperating than a woman, Zachary King had yet to meet it.

Zach was mad. Mad at his wife for her latest silly notion. She wanted to traipse up into the high country, just the two of them, and spend a week alone together. She had first suggested the trip several weeks ago, and when Zach did not respond, she had brought it up several more times, until finally she had announced they were going, and that was that.

Zach was mad at himself. Mad that he had not spoken, mad that he had not told her he had no real desire to spend a week up in the mountains when they had a perfectly good and comfortable cabin. Mad that she took it for granted he would go without even asking if he wanted to. But most of all, Zach was mad that his wife wanted to do it because of something he had said—and for the life of him, he could not remember what it was.

Zach had only himself to blame. One day some weeks past, his wife had been prattling away, as women were wont to do, and he had not been paying attention, as men were wont to do, and she had asked him a question and he had answered yes, without having any idea what she had asked.

"Consarn all women, anyhow," Zach grumbled aloud as he walked to the corral at the side of their cabin. Out on the lake a large fish jumped, but he paid it no heed. Fishing was the last thing on his mind. He was determined to solve the riddle of his wife's strange insistence on the trip to the high country.

If only he could remember! A hundred times Zach had cursed his stupidity in not paying attention that day. As best he could recollect, they had been talking about his father and mother, and what it had been like raising him and his younger sister in the remote vastness of the Rocky Mountains. But what could that possibly have to do with anything?

Zach was so deep in thought that he did not notice the rider on the white mare until the man drew rein and addressed him.

"How now, Horatio Junior? Your brow appears most unseemly troubled this fine day."

At the first word Zach had instinctively whirled and started to level his Hawken. Now he jerked the rifle down and snapped, "You can call me Zach, my white name. Or you can call me Stalking Coyote, my Shoshone name. But one name you are not to call me is Horatio Junior."

Shakespeare McNair chuckled. He had hair as

white as his mare and a beard to match, and enough wrinkles to justify his eighty-plus years. But the playful twinkle in his eyes belied his age, as did his fluid ease in dismounting and turning to the younger man. "My, my. Isn't someone in a mood today?"

"Sheath that barbed tongue of yours," Zach said.

"What a blunt fellow is this grown to be," Shakespeare quoted, looking at the mare when he said it.

"You would be grumpy too if you were me," Zach said. He had the dark hair and swarthy features of his Shoshone mother but the green eyes and broad shoulders of his white father. He wore beaded buckskins a lot like McNair's, and moccasins. Wedged under his wide leather belt were a pair of flintlock pistols, slanted across his chest were a powder horn, ammo pouch, and possibles bag. "My wife is about to drag me off into the high country."

"So I heard," Shakespeare said, for once not quoting the Bard. He placed the stock of his Hawken on the ground and leaned on the barrel. "The missus told me. She sent me over to ask if your missus wants her to water your indoor plants while you are away."

"Why didn't Blue Water Woman come herself?" Zach asked.

"How long have you been married?" Shakespeare teased. "You should know by now that a female never does anything she can get a male to do. Since all I was doing was honing an axe, she figured she could put me to better use."

"Women!" Zach spat. "If I live to be a hundred I

will never understand them."

"Don't even try," Shakespeare advised. "The Almighty put them on this earth to beguile us with their wiles and confound us with logic that is anything but logical."

"I figured if anyone would know what women are about, it would be you," Zach said. "You're almost as old as Methuselah."

Shakespeare made a show of sputtering. "I am well acquainted with your manner of wrenching the true cause the false way," he quoted. "Age has nothing to do with it, stripling. It is simply that men are men and women are women and never the twain shall meet."

"When you talk like that," Zach said, "I have no idea what you are saying."

"Perhaps I should lend you my volume on old William S."

Zach was surprised. McNair's collected works of the Bard of Avon was his most prized possession. "You would do that? You would trust me with it?"

"So long as I am with you when you read it, yes." Shakespeare grinned.

"I should have known." Zach sighed and opened the gate to the corral. "Louisa is inside if you want to ask her about the plants. Me, I have fretting to do."

"I wouldn't worry," Shakespeare said. "It will work out. Look at your father and mother."

About to step into the corral, Zach paused. "What are you talking about?"

"It is a momentous decision, yes," Shakespeare said. "But it's not like you are the first. The human race would have come to an ignoble end long ago if that were the case."

"Wait a minute," Zach said. "Are you saying that you know why Lou wants to drag me up into the mountains?"

Shakespeare blinked and blinked again, then grinned. "Are you saying that you don't?"

"Why are you looking at me like that?"

McNair snorted and started to laugh but caught himself. "For real and for true? You have no clue?"

"It's not the least bit funny," Zach said. "If you know, you must tell me or I'll be in a pickle."

"You already are," Shakespeare responded, and cackling merrily, he slapped his thigh. "Oh, this is precious. Wait until I tell your father. We all do chuckleheaded things from time to time, but this, boy, beats anything your father or I ever did, all hollow."

"I am not amused."

"I sure am," Shakespeare said, and laughed some more. "At last I realize why youth is squandered on the young. It's to give old coons like me something to laugh about."

Zach sniffed, then adopted a hurt expression. "All these years I have been calling you my uncle even though we are not blood kin, and you go and treat me like this. I expected better of you."

Shakespeare shook his head. "A fine try. But appealing to my affection won't work. You have dug a trench and jumped in feet first, and I, for one, can't wait for the trench walls to come tumbling down."

"Speak sense, will you?"

Just then the cabin door opened and out came the apple of Zach's eye. Louisa King was slender to the point of boyish, but her lustrous sandy hair, sparkling blue eyes, and lithe grace more than made up for her less than ample bosom. She was pretty, exceedingly so, even dressed in buckskins. "Shakespeare!" she squealed in delight, and came over to give him a warm hug. "I thought I heard your voice."

McNair showed more teeth than a politician giving an election speech. "Dang, girl! It's good for these old eyes to see you again. You and this contrary he-cat of yours have been keeping to yourselves too much of late." Grinning, he winked and added, "Which is understandable, all things considered."

Lou blushed and gave him a swat on the arm. "Behave, or I will inform on you to your wife."

"I wouldn't want that," Shakespeare bantered. "She might take it into her head to lift my hair." He abruptly changed the subject. "How long do you aim to be gone?"

Lou brushed at her bangs. "A couple of weeks should be enough. I want him to relax and enjoy himself while we're up there, but you know how he gets."

"Yes, I surely do," Shakespeare said with exaggerated sympathy. "How you put up with him, I will never know."

"I'm right here," Zach said.

"Good," Lou replied. "Then I won't need to repeat myself. I would like to be ready to go in an hour. If we push, we can reach that ridge where we had our picnic a while back before night sets in."

"And where a wolverine nearly had us for supper," Zach reminded her.

Lou put her hands on her hips. "You sure do grumble a lot about trifles."

"Being ripped apart and eaten is a trifle?"

"It's called being male," Shakespeare said to Louisa.

"It's called being a natural-born grump," Lou amended. "My husband isn't satisfied unless he is complaining."

Zach had started into the corral but stopped. "I will have you know my mother thinks I have a sunny disposition."

"She lied. Mothers do that." Lou started to turn to go back into the cabin, but his expression stopped her. "What?"

"My mother would never speak with two tongues," Zach said indignantly. "She is the most honest woman I know."

"Thank you ever so much," Lou said dryly. "But it won't work."

"What won't?"

"Trying to get me mad at you so I'll change my mind about our holiday," Lou said. "We're going and that is final."

"But I didn't—" Zach went to protest.

"Oh, I see right through you," Lou said. "You have regretted agreeing ever since we had our little talk, and now you want to weasel out of your promise. But I am holding you to it, come what may." Her back as stiff as a ramrod, she marched inside and slammed the door.

"You handled that well," Shakespeare said dryly.

Zach glared, then bit his lower lip and said more to himself than to McNair, "I wish I knew what I agreed to."

"Would you like a hint?" Shakespeare asked.

Zach placed his hands on the top rail. "I would be in your debt."

Shakespeare drew himself up to his full height. With a hand on his chest, he quoted, "This mock of his hath turned his balls to gun-stones."

Zach waited, and when no more was forthcoming, said, "What kind of hint is that? It makes no more sense than anything else your namesake wrote."

Ordinarily quick to take offense at a slight against his idol, Shakespeare merely grinned. "It will, stripling. It will. And when it does, I hope you look back and remember and find it half as humorous as I do." Chuckling, he led his mare over to tie her but paused when hoofs thudded and around the corner of the cabin swept a large man on a large bay.

"Pa!" Zach said happily.

Nate King was dressed in buckskins much like those of his son and his best friend. Like them, too, he was a living armory; pistols, knife, tomahawk, and rifle were his weapons of choice. His long hair and beard were raven black, his features so composed that most women would rate him handsome. He smiled warmly at Zach and Shakespeare as he swung down from his saddle. "Glad I caught you before Lou and you rode off."

"Something on your mind?" Zach asked, hoping there was, hoping his father needed him to go to Bent's Fort for provisions or maybe to hunt meat for their respective larders. *Anything* to get him out of going up into the high country.

Nate placed his big hand on his son's shoulder. "I just wanted to wish you well. This is a big step you're taking."

At that juncture Shakespeare stepped forward and whispered in Nate's ear, but loud enough for Zach to hear, "Horatio Junior has no notion what it is about."

"How is that?" Nate quizzically asked.

McNair nodded at Zach, and snickered. "Your boy is in a fog about why his wife wants to drag him up into the mountains."

"No," Nate King said.

"Yes," Shakespeare confirmed.

Nate stared at the fruit of his loins. "Is this true?"

"I'm a mite confused," Zach admitted. "You see, we were talking one day, and I wasn't paying as much attention as maybe I should have—" He got no further. His father was bent over, laughing. "Why does everyone find this so hysterical?"

"Heavens make our presence and our practices pleasant and helpful to him," Shakespeare quoted.

"What is it, Pa?" Zach asked. "What do you and Uncle Shakespeare know that I don't?"

"A lot of things," Shakespeare answered before Nate could. "But pertinent to the moment is this." He paused, then quoted, "Two hot sheeps, marry."

Nate laughed harder.

"What do sheep have to do with it?" Zach demanded. He was close to losing his temper.

"Nothing, since you were not counting them," Shakespeare said, then once again quoted his namesake, "You find not the apostrophes, and so miss the accent."

Zach clenched his fists. "If I listen to much more of this, my head will explode." Wheeling, he stalked toward the horses on the other side of the corral.

"Should we enlighten him?" Shakespeare asked.

Nate shook his head. "He is old enough to wipe his own feet. Let him find out the hard way. Maybe it will teach him to listen when his wife talks to him."

"Not that we have ever been guilty of the offense," Shakespeare said, his seamed faced curled in a lopsided smirk. "I try, I truly try, but most of it goes in one ear and bounces out again."

"Ever confessed that to Blue Water Woman?" Nate inquired.

"And have her take a rolling pin to my head? No, thank you. That woman has picked up a lot of white ways she could do without. Most Flathead gals don't give their husbands half the sass she gives me. I have told her that, too."

"Your wife and my wife are of the opinion you deserve it," Nate commented. "They were talking the other day when Blue Water Woman came over for tea, and I happened to be outside the window and heard every word."

"Just happened to be there, huh?" Shakespeare said, then recoiled as if he had been pricked with a pin. "Did you say *deserved* to be sassed?"

Nate nodded.

"How did those contrary females come to that conclusion?" Shakespeare asked in a mild huff.

"It had to do with you always quoting old Willy

S.," Nate said, and scratched his chin. "Let me think. What was it your wife said?" He snapped his fingers. "Now I remember. She said that if she had to put up with living with a talking book, you shouldn't quibble over a tiny bit of sass." Nate grinned. " 'Tiny bit.' Her exact words."

Shakespeare's mouth was moving, but no words came out. Finally he uttered a cross between a bark and a bleat and shook his rifle as if he yearned to brain someone with it. "A pox on her and all her kind! Her kisses are Judas's own children! Women stab us in the back and call it a favor."

"I think you are overreacting."

"Which shows how much you know about women!" Shakespeare blustered. "They are catamounts in skirts, and not to be trusted."

As if to prove his point, Louisa came striding out of the cabin with a pistol in her hand. "Where is that no-account husband of mine? I aim to blow out his wick and be done with him."

Chapter Two

"I rest my case," Shakespeare McNair said.

"What has you so riled?" Nate asked his daughter-in-law, but she stomped past him to the corral, her jaw muscles twitching.

Zach came to the open gate leading a sorrel.

"Dang," Shakespeare said. "I wish I had some jerky. I could sit down and enjoy this. It's better than watching bull elk in rut."

Nate arched an eyebrow. "At your age. You ought to be ashamed of yourself."

"I meant the fighting, not the other," Shakespeare said, "but now that you mention it, what do you think keeps me so young and handsome?"

"Thank you. I will carry that image around in my head for the rest of the day and won't be able to touch food."

"Only the rest of the day?" Shakespeare countered, then raised a finger. "Hush now. It's about to get interesting."

Over at the corral, Lou was shaking the pistol at Zach. "I can't believe it! I can't believe you deliberately ignored me."

Unsure over what she was incensed about, Zach asked, "What did I do now?"

"Don't take that tone with me, mister," Lou said. "You know very well what you did. Or, rather, didn't do. Last night I asked you to pack the pemmican and other things I wanted to take along and you told me you would. But I just opened the cupboard, and lo and behold, you didn't pack a lick."

"I forgot," Zach said.

Lou stamped a small foot. "Do my requests mean so little to you? What happened to the days when you doted on my every word?"

Shakespeare nudged Nate and whispered, "Oh, this is a good one. It appears the luster has worn off the peach."

"Be nice," Nate said.

Zach tied the sorrel to a rail and turned to his wife. He was uncomfortable arguing with his father and uncle right there. Then, too, he and Lou rarely fought. He truly was devoted to her, even if at times she drove him to distraction. "You can't blame me. It's your fault I forgot."

"Me?" Lou cried.

Shakespeare chuckled and whispered. "Oh! Did you hear that? Your boy is brilliant. Parry and thrust, parry and thrust, that's the way to keep them off their guard."

"Will you shush?"

"How can it be my fault?" Lou protested. "I asked, you said you would, you didn't. It's that simple."

Zach cradled his rifle in his arms and calmly rebutted, "Who was it came up to me while I was stoking the fire and put her arms around me? Who was it nibbled on my ear?"

"He's wonderful," Shakespeare whispered to Nate. "Taken the guilt off his shoulders and draped it over hers. See her fidget? Sharp as a tack, that boy. I am proud to be his uncle."

"He only calls you that," Nate said irritably. "You are no blood relation whatsoever."

"That was mean-spirited," Shakespeare said. "You're upset because your boy is better at holding his own with females than you are."

"I can hold my own with Winona, thank you very much."

"Ha. Quite the jester. She wears you like a ring. You are wrapped around her little finger, hers to command as she pleases."

Nate frowned. "I will have you know—" he began, forgetting to whisper.

"Quiet, will you?" Shakespeare cut him off. "A second sally is under way and I would rather listen to them."

"I could just shoot you sometimes."

Zach placed his hand on Lou's shoulder and tenderly squeezed. "If I've hurt your feelings, I am sorry. But I didn't do it on purpose. Hurting you is the last thing I would ever do."

Shakespeare poked Nate again. "Did you hear? A genius at work, I tell you. Of course, that only works early in a marriage. Before all the romance dries up."

"You haven't seen a club lying around, have you?"

Lou embraced Zach. "I'm sorry. It's just that this is so important to me. I want it more than anything, Zachary, and I am grateful you have agreed. It means the world to me." She pecked his cheek. "Don't worry about the packing. I'll take care of it." Smiling over her shoulder, she went indoors.

Zach stared after her. More than ever, he wished he could recall the talk they had. He tried once more to remember and was only dimly aware that Shakespeare had come over until a brawny hand clapped him on the back.

"Congratulations, pup. Nicely done, if I say so myself." Shakespeare launched into another quote. "Praise him that got thee, she that gave thee suck. Famed be thy tutor." He grinned. "That would be me."

Zach regarded him a moment, then his father, who had joined them. "Enough tomfoolery. I really need to know."

"We have milked it dry, I suppose," Shakespeare said. "Although if I tried, I could squeeze out a few more drops of humor."

Nate self-consciously cleared his throat. "Son, Lou is excited because you finally agreed to start the family she has always wanted."

"I did what?"

"You heard the man," Shakespeare tittered. "The treasure of your eye and you were riding one day. Apparently she said something about wanting to have a baby and you agreed. Or so my wife says your wife told her."

Zach took a step back. "Dear God."

"You had no idea?" Nate asked.

"None," Zach breathed, astounded by his lapse. "This can't be. It just can't be."

Shakespeare snorted. "You make it sound like she wants you to wrestle a griz. Making a tyke can be fun. It is the one time women don't gripe if you want to do it in the middle of the afternoon."

"People do that?" Nate said.

Zach shook his head. "No, you don't understand, either of you. I'm not ready to have children."

"When will you be ready? When you are as old as me?" Shakespeare asked. "Hellfire, boy. Have them while you are young and can keep up with their antics, because when you are my age, the creaking in your joints slows you down considerable."

"He has a point," Nate said. "Have your children now rather than ten years from now. Space them a few years apart so they can grow up together. Children need other children."

"That they do," Shakespeare agreed. "Not that there is anything wrong with being a solitary, but it helps them get along with others."

"Aren't either of you listening?" Zack asked. "I'm not ready to have kids. The notion scares me."

"You'll be a fine father," Nate said.

"Of course you will," Shakespeare echoed. "You have your father and me as examples."

"You don't have children," Zach reminded him.

Shakespeare's features clouded. "Blue Water Woman and I came together too late in life for that to be practical."

"What about with your first wife? The one the Blackfeet killed," Zach asked. "What was her name again? Rainbow Woman?"

If a man's countenance could reflect inexpressible sorrow, Shakespeare's did. "Yes. My first love. They say our first loves are out dearest and truest and that we never forget them." A sigh was torn from the depths of his soul. "I sure haven't."

"Doesn't Blue Water Woman mind?" Zach wondered. "You caring for Rainbow Woman so much?"

A shiver seemed to pass through McNair, but then he steadied himself and looked up. "How little you know of the female persuasion. Women don't mind competition if the competition is dead."

Zach noticed his father giving him a certain look, and quickly said, "It was stupid of me to bring that up. I'm sorry."

"We can't hide from our hurts," Shakespeare said. "Especially the ones that cut to the heart."

"Was that another quote from Willy S.?" Zach sought to make light of it.

"No, that was me," Shakespeare responded with a wry grin. "Now and again I have a glimmer."

Zach turned to his father. "About this baby business, what am I going to do?"

"Have one," Nate said.

"How many times must I repeat myself? I am not ready."

"Give us one good reason why."

"How about a handful? I'm too young. I don't know the first thing about rearing a child. I have no patience. I have a temper."

"I was younger than you when I had you," Nate said. "As for knowing what to do, you learn as you go. Just like you do everything else in life.

They call that experience. As for the rest of your objections, they are more akin to quibbles."

"Look, son," Shakespeare said. "There isn't a man been born who hasn't felt the same fear you are feeling at the thought of bringing new life into the world. It's a big responsibility, the biggest we have our entire lives, and we are afraid we won't do it right."

"You felt the same way? And, Pa, you too?"

Both men nodded.

"I was scared to death when your mother told me she was with child," Nate admitted. "I spent weeks worrying myself silly. I thought I would be the worst parent who ever drew breath."

"But you've been a fine father," Zach said.

"My point, exactly," Nate replied. "We always think we will do worse than we actually do."

"It's human nature," Shakespeare interjected. "Most folks tend to expect the worst and then are pleasantly surprised when everything turns out better than they reckoned it would."

"I still don't know," Zach said uncertainly.

"It's your decision," Nate said. "Yours, and Lou's. You've seen how happy she is. Changing your mind will crush her."

"But I never made up my mind in the first place," Zach objected. "So it is not like I would be changing it."

"Either way," Nate said, "if you tell her no, it will be the same as sticking a knife in her gut."

"And twisting the knife once it's in," Shakespeare added. His voice softened. "Women are contrary critters. But they also have their good qualities. When they love a man, when they give their heart and soul, they will do anything for him. All they ask in return is that the man respect them and love them and provide some of the niceties of life. That's not so much to ask for, is it?"

"Children are more than a nicety," Zach said.

"Children are the glue that holds a good marriage together and the thorns that tear a bad marriage apart," Shakespeare declared. "In your case they will be more glue than acid."

"You don't know that for sure."

Nate and Shakespeare exchanged looks, and McNair said, "An acorn never falls far from the tree. You are a lot like your pa, more than you are maybe willing to admit. You have a lot of your ma in you, too, which I will never embarrass you by mentioning ever again."

"So you're saying I have what it takes to be a good parent?"

Shakespeare grinned. "Took the words right out of my mouth. But that's only part of it."

"What's the other part?"

"You love that little gal with all that you are, and you will be the best father you can just to please her."

Zach walked to the open cabin door. He leaned against the jamb and watched his wife bustle about, getting ready. She was smiling and humming to herself. He had seldom seen her so radiant. Then she stepped to the counter, and a splash of light from the window played over her face. For a few breathless seconds she was the most beautiful sight he ever beheld, so beautiful that he yearned to take her in his arms and smother her lips and cheeks with hot kisses. A warm flush crept over him, and he coughed.

Louisa looked around, beaming. "You have the horses saddled already? My, that was fast."

"No, I don't," Zach said.

Lou came over. Some of her radiance faded, to be replaced by worry. "Don't tell me you don't want to do it. Not after you said you would. I have been looking forward to this so much."

"Lou—" Zach began.

"Hear me out, please," Lou said, taking his hands in hers. "I want a baby more than anything. I have nagged you about it, yes, and for that I apologize. But if you could feel how much I want one, if you could look into my heart—"

Zach held up a hand, stopping her. "I already have. Our hearts are entwined forever, remember?"

A tear formed at the corner of Lou's eye and trickled down her cheek. "Zachary King, that is the sweetest thing you have ever said to me. Does this mean I haven't been dreaming? That you really and truly want to start a family?"

Zach King gazed into his wife's blue eyes, into the loveliest eyes in all creation, and with a full understanding of what he was saying and a full appreciation of the consequences, he smiled and said, "Yes."

Lou squealed for joy and clapped her hands, then threw them around his neck and kissed him. "Thank you, thank you, thank you! Now go get the horses ready." She stared lovingly up at him. "You will like where we are going. It is somewhere you have wanted to go since we moved to this valley. It's the perfect place for us to be alone together."

"Where would that be?" Zach asked.

Louisa drew him to the doorway and pointed at a white mass on a mountain to the northwest. "The glacier."

Chapter Three

King Valley, as it later became known, was one of the largest in the central Rockies. The valley floor was lush with grass watered by sparkling runoff from on high, runoff that also fed the broad lake that had been there since the dawn of time. Or so the neighboring tribes claimed.

Wildlife was abundant. A legion of deer came to the lake to drink during the night and retreated into the thick timber during the day. Elk did the same. Occasionally, a small herd of shaggy mountain buffalo would venture to the lake but they never stayed long. Unlike their prairie brethren, they preferred shadowy thickets to open spaces. Mountain goats were visible on the rocky crags that surrounded the valley, white specks against a backdrop of brown. After the sun went down, the howls of wolves, the yips of coyotes, and the screech of mountain lions testified to the existence of the many predators seldom seen when the sun was up.

Lesser game was just as plentiful. Long-eared rabbits that bounded off in impossible leaps. Squirrels that chattered irately at anyone and anything that came near the trees they were in. Chipmunks always in dizzying motion, their tails held erect like tiny flags. Higher up were badger burrows. Beaver worked industriously in the fish-filled streams. Raccoons made nightly rounds, as did porcupines and opossums.

Not to be outdone, the avian contingent was well represented. At the top of the bird hierarchy were the bald and the golden eagles. Lords of the air, they soared high on outstretched pinions, ready to swoop down on unsuspecting prey. Hawks patrolled the grassy valley and timbered slopes alike. Owls nested in the cover of the trees while the sun was up and came out once it was down to ask their eternal question. The raucous cries of ravens made the songbirds nervous, for ravens were notorious raiders of both eggs and the chicks that hatched from those eggs. Jays pierced the crisp mountain air with their strident squawks. Splashes of vivid color betrayed the presence of robins, bluebirds, and tanagers.

As prolific as the wildlife was, it could not hold a candle to the plant life. Not one, not two, but several varieties of grass carpeted the valley floor, including the long-stemmed buffalo grass more common lower down. Columbines and daisies grew in profusion during the warm months, only two of over a dozen types of flowers that decorated the wild. Near the lake and along the streams grew oaks and cottonwoods. Groves of aspens transformed into spectacular displays of red and yellow when the weather turned. Spruce were everywhere, heartleaf and calypso not quite as common. Higher up thrived phalanxes of tall firs.

King Valley was a green and blue jewel amid the brown crags and gray cliffs. Paradise, Nate called it, and paradise it was, which made the absence of humans all the more surprising.

Indians shunned the valley. The nearest tribe, the Utes, was vehement in its belief that it was bad medicine but strangely reticent when asked why. The Shoshones and the Crows likewise would not set foot there, although their reasons for avoiding the valley were different from the mysterious reason the Utes would not share. The Flatheads and the Nez Perce lived too far away to include the valley in their annual migrations, but even they said the valley was a place of evil and must be shunned.

Not long ago, four young Crows, not intimidated by the warnings of their elders, had announced they were going to the valley to hunt elk—and were never heard from again.

Nate King respected the tribes' beliefs but he did not share them. His previous homestead, low in the foothills, had become a stopping point for travelers bound for Oregon Country and other settlers who had followed his example. Enough that Nate had begun to feel crowded. That, and the increasing absence of game, fueled his decision to uproot his family and friends and take them to this new haven deep in the mountains where they could live out the rest of their days amid Nature's bounty.

There had been difficulties. A grizzly took exception to the intrusion. The brood of a female wolverine had hunted them as they hunted other game. And an unknown tribe to the west had made a few unfriendly forays.

But all in all, life in the new valley was good.

Zach had no objections. Lou liked their new, more spacious cabin. He liked living by the lake. Day after day, they went about their usual routine. They would rise at the first blush of dawn and eat a hearty breakfast. Zach would hunt or fish or chop wood for the fireplace while Lou busied herself with the thousand and one tasks that made their cabin a home. At midday they always took a short break. The afternoons were spent in more work. Twilight signaled the end to their toil. They would eat supper, read or talk awhile, and turn in early. The next day the pattern was repeated.

Zach rarely gave any thought to the talk among the tribes about the bad medicine. He took it for granted, as did his father and McNair, that the bad medicine referred to the hostiles to the west. And since his father had closed the pass to the next valley, the hostiles no longer posed a threat.

Still . . .

Hostiles did not explain the sounds that occasionally wafted their way on the night wind. From out of the northwest the sounds came, howls that were not howls and shrieks that were not shrieks. Ululating cries such as Zach had never heard. Nor his father. Nor McNair. They would hear the eerie cries and stop whatever they were doing to listen, racking their brains for an explanation.

Zach, in particular, was fascinated by the cries. It had to be an animal, but what kind? It wasn't a wolf or a coyote or a cougar. Bears were incapable of making such sounds. In his more fanciful musings, Zach imagined it to be some new animal awaiting discovery.

Zach could not establish what it was, but he did establish one fact: The cries came from the vicinity of the glacier. Which tied in with the Ute taboo. The Utes would never say exactly why the valley was bad medicine, but they had let it slip that it had something to do with the glacier.

To complicate matters, on some nights the sounds were different than on others. On some nights, from the rising of the moon until the rising of the sun, the valley's peace was shattered by unceasing roars that cowed every creature which heard them. Strangely enough, to Zach it did not seem as if the roars came from the same throat that gave voice to the howls and shrieks. It was almost enough to make him think there were two "somethings" up there, but that was absurd.

The matter was very much on his mind as Zach and Louisa forked leather and prepared to ride off. Zach held the lead rope to their packhorse. His Hawken was slung across his back. "We are going," he said, which was a silly statement since his father and Shakespeare could plainly see they were ready.

"Take care up there," McNair urged. "Keep your eyes skinned and your powder dry."

Nate smiled at Lou. "Don't you worry about your plants. Winona has promised to water them. And I'll take care of your chickens and the pigs."

"Thank you. The sow is due soon. Watch her. She bites sometimes." Louisa smiled and gestured at the ring of towering peaks. "I am in heaven. We haven't had much time to ourselves since we moved here."

"Enjoy yourself."

"That goes without saying," Lou replied, and lowered her voice so Zach would not hear. "If all goes well, nine months from now Winona and you will have those grandchildren you have wanted."

"Don't do it on our account," Nate said. "Only if you are hankering to change diapers."

Louisa chuckled. "I've been ready for a couple of years now. It's that stubborn son of yours who always balks."

Zach twisted in his saddle. "What was that? Are you two talking about me again?"

"Not everything is about you, one I love," Lou impishly returned. "Some of us can go a whole day without mentioning you."

"Women," Zach said.

"Men," Lou retorted.

Shakespeare winked at Nate. "If these two were any more loving, you would think they were enemies."

"You don't fool anyone," Louisa said. "Not after what your wife has told us. You are more romantic than all of us combined."

"Yes," Zach said. "What was that about you

posing in the altogether with a flower in your teeth?"

Shakespeare McNair turned the same color as a beet. "Blue Water Woman told you *that*?"

"And more," Louisa said.

"The woman is a fiend!" Shakespeare declared. "Such an injury would vex a saint."

"Saint McNair," Zach said, and laughed.

"You find that humorous?"

"I seem to recollect that to be a saint, you have to be as pure as the driven snow. Unless the snow is black, you wouldn't qualify."

McNair roared with glee. "By jove, Horatio Junior, that was a good one. My wit is beginning to rub off on you."

"Just so a little of that romance rubs off on him as well," Lou remarked, regarding her husband adoringly.

"Time to leave," Zach said.

Nate and Shakespeare stood looking after them until they entered the trees. Zach turned and waved and his father waved back. Then the vegetation closed around them.

The ground was level until they came to the base of the mountain to the northwest. There it sloped upward, gradually at first but ever steeper as they climbed. It was a challenge to both rider and mount. Now and again, when they crossed open areas, Zach would tilt his head back and stare at the whitish-blue relict far above.

At midday they stopped to rest the horses. Lou opened a parfleche and gave Zach pemmican. She had made it herself, adding extra berries as he liked. She sat on a log to eat and he sank down beside her.

"We don't have to go to the glacier, you know."

Lou stopped chewing in surprise. "What?"

"We don't have to go all the way to the glacier," Zach repeated. "It will take days to get there."

"But you've wanted to see it since we came," Lou noted. "I thought you would leap at the chance."

Zach shrugged. "I've never seen a glacier close-up before. But it seems a shame to waste days we could better spend relaxing in a meadow some-where."

"What is this?" Lou asked. "Why the sudden change of mind?"

"No reason," Zach said.

"Liar. You're thinking of those sounds we hear. Thinking that whatever makes them might be dangerous."

"Can I help it if I don't want any harm to come to you?" Zach countered. "It's bad enough we are constantly running into bears and whatnot."

Lou tenderly touched his cheek. "It's sweet of you to be so concerned." She patted the flintlocks tucked under her belt and the rifle propped on the log next to her leg. "But I can take care of myself."

"I never said you couldn't," Zach said. "Why invite grief, though, if there is no reason?"

"I can't believe my ears," Lou said. "You, of all people, shying from possible trouble?"

"So?"

"So you have spent your whole life courting trouble, not running from it. You get into more scrapes than anyone I know."

"That's different," Zach said. "I never start those scrapes. Usually I'm minding my own business and the Blackfeet or someone else comes along and wants to separate me from my hair."

"Danger is danger, and you thrive on it."

Zach wagged a piece of pemmican at her. "Shows how much you know. I didn't do much thriving that time that grizzly drove me over a cliff. Or that time the wolverine jumped me."

"You know what I mean." Lou's lovely blue eyes narrowed. "You really don't want to go all the way to the glacier?"

Zach was quiet a bit, chewing. "I heard it last night."

"What?"

"What have we been talking about? The thing up near the glacier. You were snoring and I couldn't sleep so I stepped outside for some fresh air and I heard its cries."

"And now you are having second thoughts."

"The moon is full. We always hear it more when the moon is full."

"But the moon won't be full by the time we get there," Lou noted.

"All I'm saying is that we don't have to go there if you find a spot you like on the way up."

Lou shifted and peered through the trees but could not see the white mass. "Aren't you curious, though? I am. I'd like to know what makes those sounds. What if it *is* dangerous? What then?"

"All the more reason we should leave it alone," Zach said.

"You're missing my point. What if it is dangerous and it decides to pay us a visit some night? Say, after our baby is born. Wouldn't it be better to find out what it is now rather than later?"

Zach had not thought of that and admitted as much.

"We don't need to decide now. We can decide when we get up higher. But I think we should have a look-see."

That evening they camped on a ridge covered with aspens. Zach kindled a fire and Lou cooked supper. They had plenty of provisions, enough to last a month if need be. She had brought a slab of venison from a buck Zach shot two days ago. She cut the meat into strips, then put them in a pan on a flat rock near the flames. In another pan she mixed chopped carrots with chopped onions. In a third she mixed cornmeal, water, and sugar to make a johnnycake. She reached for a spoon and froze.

Zach heard it, too. The crackle of the undergrowth. Something was coming toward them. He grabbed his Hawken and whirled just as the animal, grunting and snorting, came barreling into the open.

Chapter Four

Zach thought it was a bear. The grunts and the snorts were typical of the sounds a bear made. But to his bemusement, and relief, it was a creature far less formidable.

"It's only a porky," Louisa said, wagging the spoon. "It scared me out of a year's growth."

The porcupine stopped. Normally, porcupines avoided humans. This one grunted and started and sniffed, then did the last thing Zach expected; it kept coming.

"What in blazes?" Zach raised the Hawken to his shoulder and curled his thumb around the hammer.

"Don't shoot it," Louisa said. "It can't do any harm and we don't need the meat." She giggled girlishly. "It's sort of cute, don't you think?"

Zach thought no such thing. With their long barbed quills, blunt heads, squat bodies, and short legs, they had to be the ugliest creatures alive. They were good eating, though. Shakespeare was partial to porcupine meat, and had served it when he had them over for supper.

The porcupine came to within about six feet of them, and stopped.

"What do you suppose it wants?" Lou wondered.

"It smells the food," Zach guessed. "Or it wants our salt." Porcupines craved salt like some men craved whiskey. He wagged the Hawken at it. "Shoo! Go away, you blamed nuisance."

The porcupine just stood there.

"Maybe I should give it some salt and it will go away," Lou suggested.

"It will only want more," Zach said. He took a step and poked his rifle at its snout. "Do your ears work? Get out of here before I give you a boot in the backside."

"I wouldn't, were I you," Lou said. "I hear the quills hurt like the dickens and are awful hard to get out."

Zach knew all about those quills. Once, years ago, his mother had taken them to visit her people. The Shoshones—or the Snakes, as the whites called them—were camped near the Green River. Their first night there, some of the dogs put up a racket. The next morning Zach was strolling about the village when he saw a small crowd and heard a dog whine. He went over and saw that one of the dogs had half a dozen quills sticking from its mouth and face. A porcupine had wandered into the village and the dogs had driven it off. Now the dog's owner was trying to pull the quills out, without much success. The quills were embedded deep, the barbs caught fast. The warrior pulled and pulled but they would not come out. Finally it was decided to cut the quills and dig out the barbs, but as soon as the man began prying with his knife, the dog yelped and jerked back and would not let him try again. Three days later the dog's face was swollen to twice its normal size. By the sixth day, its face was a mass of festering sores that oozed pus and reeked terribly. On the twelfth day the dog died.

"Watch out!" Lou cried.

The porcupine had turned its back to Zach and was backing toward him, its quills bristling like so many short spears. He quickly sidestepped and poked it with the Hawken, only to have it turn and back toward him again, this time swinging its tail.

"Be careful!"

Zach retreated. He had no desire to kill it. He was surprised more than anything else. Springing to the right to avoid a sweep of the nearly foot-long tail, he jabbed at it again with his rifle.

"You're only making it mad," Lou said.

With surprising speed, the porcupine darted in close and swung its tail at Zach's left ankle. He leaped clear, but only just, and this time gave it a hard whack with the stock. "Go pester someone else, damn you!"

Lou watched his antics with an amused smirk. "Well, that will certainly calm it down."

Zach was growing mad, but not at the porcupine, at her. Instead of helping, she was making stupid comments. He was about to give her a piece of his mind when suddenly the porcupine came at him again. Backpedaling, he tripped, and before he could stop himself, he fell on his side with his face barely a foot from their unwanted visitor.

Lou screamed.

The porcupine was quick to seize the advantage. With a loud grunt it jumped at Zach's face, its bristling quills extended. Zach barely swung his rifle between them in time. As it was several quills scraped his knuckles, drawing blood but not penetrating.

A pistol boomed.

At the blast, the porcupine lurched and stumbled, the top of its head disappearing in a spray of quills, bone, and gore. It twitched a few times, then was still.

Zach slowly rose. "I thought you didn't want it killed."

"I changed my mind," Lou said, and blew a puff of breath at the smoke curling from the muzzle of her flintlock. "It darned near took your eyes out."

"Strange, it acting like it did," Zach said, and nudged the prickly form with the Hawken. "Want me to cut it up?"

"Just bury it," Lou said.

Zach looked around. It was not like her to waste good meat. "Are you sure? I can dry the meat and salt it."

"I'm sure," Lou said. She commenced reloading.

Zach filled with pride. She was a fine wife. It was funny how life worked out. He always thought he would spend his life a bachelor. The idea of being tied to a woman and a home for the rest of his days had held little appeal. He had seen himself wandering the frontier, having one grand adventure after another. How silly those thoughts seemed now. How childish. Because now that he was married, he could not imagine himself alone. Specifically, he could not imagine his life without Lou.

She had become everything to him. That she put up with him was a marvel. He was the first to concede he was not easy to live with. He had a temper, for one thing. For another, he was not as neat and tidy as most women liked their men to be. For yet another, he had barely a thimble's full of patience. He carped a lot. He tended to regard everyone as an enemy until they proved otherwise. As he saw it, the list of his faults was longer than his arm, yet she did not seem to mind.

Then there was her looks. To Zach she was the most beautiful woman who ever lived. Which, in a way, was peculiar, since he knew women with bigger bosoms and shapelier figures. Yet to him, she was lovelier than all of them, and when he first met her, he could not say why she so appealed to him.

Zach had thought about it a lot since, and he had come to the conclusion it was Lou, herself, and not her hair or her lips or her hips, which so stirred him. It was her personality, her spirit, the part of her that was *her*, to which the part of him that was him responded.

Zach could remember when he was seven or eight. One day he heard his father tell his mother that he loved her, just as his father had done countless times. But on that occasion Zach had looked up from his oatmeal and asked, "Pa, what is love?"

His father had looked at him and said, "You are a little young to be asking a question like that."

"Answer him, husband," Winona said from over by the stove. "I would like to hear."

"Love is a lot of things," Nate had said. "Love is when you care for someone more than you care for yourself. Love is when you want to do all you can to make the other person happy." His father had paused. "But most of all, love is a special warmth deep inside."

Zach never forgot those words. They stuck in his mind, stuck with him as he grew, and then one day he met Lou and the words came back to him in a rush of feeling. He cared for her more than anything, and wanted more than anything to make her happy.

"Are you going to bury it or stand there with that silly look on your face?"

The question snapped Zach out of his reverie. Lou had finished reloading and was hunkered by the frying pans. "I was thinking," he said.

"What about?"

Zach hesitated. He was never entirely comfortable talking about his feelings. He could tell her he loved her, he would sometimes whisper endearments in the quiet of the night, but that was the extent of it. To delve deeper was just not in him. He was not Shakespeare. Wonderful words did not trip lightly off his tongue. Often he had to wrestle with himself to find the right thing to say. Like now. "How lucky I am that I met you."

"You are a dear," Lou said affectionately.

Zach bent to grab the porcupine and drag it off, then realized what he was doing. He went in

search of a downed tree branch and found a suitable limb under a pine. As thick as his arm and
twice as long, it sufficed to roll the porcupine
away to a spot at the edge of the darkness. The
ground was hard and he had not brought a shovel.
There again, the limb was stout enough for him to
use it to break the earth into clods and scrape out
a shallow oval. He flipped the body into the hole,
covered it, and stamped the dirt down.

Lou had a cup of hot coffee waiting. He liked
his coffee black. He gulped half to wash down the
dust of the trail, then sat back and sighed. The
warmth in his belly, the warmth of the fire, the
warmth in his wife's eyes, they filled him with a
rare sense of peace and contentment.

Always sensitive to his moods, Lou asked,
"Why did you sigh?"

"Just happy, I guess," Zach answered.

"It means a lot to me, your doing this."

"So you have made plain," Zach said. "And
maybe you are right. Maybe it is time we started a
family."

"Maybe? I thought you had made up your
mind. I thought you wanted this as much as I do."

"I do, I do," Zach said. He was wary of spoil-
ing her mood. Women were temperamental that
way. "I wouldn't have agreed if I didn't want to
have one."

Lou opened her mouth to say something, and
turned to stone.

The wind had picked up, as it almost always
did at night, gusting strong from the northwest.
Earlier it had carried with it the yip of a lonesome
coyote. Once they heard the bleat of an animal

caught by a predator. Now the wind brought to their ears a wavering howl. It rose to a piercing screech, then faded to a rumble like that of a bear, only this was no bear.

"The glacier beast!" Lou exclaimed

The short hairs at the nape of Zach's neck prickled. They did nearly every time he heard it. Right then and there he made up his mind that under no circumstances were they climbing all the way to the glacier. He would find a place to stop long before they got there and concoct an excuse she would accept.

The cry died. They listened awhile but it was not repeated.

Lou was disappointed. "Your father once told me there are creatures in these mountains we know little about. Creatures the Indians say were here before they came. Creatures that should have died out long ago."

"My mother's people and other tribes have many legends," Zach said. "When I was little I would sit on Touch the Cloud's knee and hear about the time when all the animals were much bigger than they are now. Some were hairy, like buffalo. Others had horns in the middle of their heads. There were cats as big as bears, their teeth as long as sabers."

"Do you believe all that?" Lou asked.

"The Indians do. It has been passed down from father to son for more winters than anyone can count."

"You think the thing up at the glacier is one of those creatures?"

"I wouldn't go that far. But there is a quote

Shakespeare is fond of." Zach had to think before it came to him. "There are more things in heaven and on earth than are dreamt of in our philosophy. Or something like that."

"Whatever it is, we might be the first to set eyes on it," Lou said. "Wouldn't that be exciting?"

Zach smiled, but he did not feel excited. He did not feel excited at all. When they turned in, he lay on his back with his head on his hands and listened for the cry to come again, but whatever made it was silent.

The next day was a repeat of the first. Except for short rests they spent every minute in the saddle, climbing, always climbing. Talus became common. So did slopes littered with boulders, some the size of a log cabin. Blue spruce thrived, the tallest over eighty feet high. A belt of gambel oak was unexpected. A belt of aspens was not. Cottonwoods bordered the stream fed by the glacier, the stream Zach had been paralleling since they left the valley floor. The stream followed a meandering course, as mountain waterways were wont to do, flowing in the path of least resistance.

Lou was all for striking off overland to the glacier, but Zach talked her out of it. "We should stay close to water for the horses' sake." He had another reason, one he did not share.

That night they camped in the lee of a hummock. It sheltered them from the worst of the wind and hid their fire from prying eyes higher up. Lou did not think of that, but Zach did. Zach thought, too, of scattering dry twigs around their camp so that if anything came near, they were

bound to hear. He scattered the twigs while Lou
was busy washing the supper dishes.

The third day Zach again made it a point to
stay close to the stream. He often rode with his
gaze glued to the ground and not to the slope
above. If Lou noticed, she did not comment on it.
But she was sure to guess why.

Water was life. Without it, wildlife perished.
Every animal, from the smallest to the largest,
came to where water was to be found. Some only
came once a day. Some came more often. Deer
liked to drink at dawn and again at dusk. So did
elk. Mountain buffalo drank during the heat of
the day and then retired into the timber. Rabbits,
squirrels, even mice, everything came to drink,
and everything left tracks.

It was the middle of the afternoon when Zach
rounded a bend and drew rein at a gravel bar. He
had found what he was looking for.

"Why did you stop?" Lou asked, gigging her
dun up next to him.

Zach pointed.

Lou glanced at the gravel bar and gave a start.
"What in God's name made those?"

"I wish to God I knew."

Chapter Five

There were two tracks. Just the two, where something had leaped from the bank, landed in the middle of the gravel bar, and then apparently bounded into the stream and on across it. To judge by the distance from the bank to the prints, whatever made them had jumped over twelve feet. To reach the other side would take another jump of ten feet. Zach doubted he could do it, even with a running start.

Another aspect to the tracks was even more disturbing. Their outline was vaguely human, but the clear imprint of claws suggested they were clearly not. The left foot also had a spur or bulge for which Zach could not account. He placed his foot next to one of the prints, and whistled. His was dwarfed. The tracks were three to four inches longer and two to three inches wider.

Lou was just as impressed. "Whatever made those was huge."

Zach hunkered. He ran his fingers along the edge of each track and then placed his palm flat in one. The edges were not well defined and the bottom was pockmarked with tiny circles. "These are old. It's rained since they were made, and it hasn't rained for weeks."

"How long ago, exactly?" Lou wanted to know.

"A month or more," was Zach's best deduction. Straightening, he thoughtfully regarded the white mass of ice up near the mountain's summit. "We're miles away yet."

"Maybe there will be more sign the closer we get."

"Maybe we shouldn't get any closer."

Lou looked at him. "Why not? You want to know what made them, don't you? I certainly do."

"Some things are better left alone," Zach said.

"That sounds like something your father would say," Lou responded. "The man I married should be bubbling with curiosity right about now. He would never pass up a chance to investigate something like this."

"The man you married is worried about the woman he married."

"Why? We have our guns. We have our knives. What can harm us?"

"A lot of things." Zach scanned the gravel bar for other tracks, but there were none. "Grizzlies, mountain lions, wolverines, wolves, rattlesnakes, hostiles, rabid chipmunks."

A snort burst from Louisa. "Rabid chipmunks? Now you're reaching. And need I remind you that the woman you married can take care of herself?"

"So she keeps saying," Zach said. "And need I

remind her that she is flesh and bone just like everyone else, and flesh and bone can be clawed to shreds?"

Lou regarded him with a half smile. "All right. Who are you and what have you done with my husband? Where is the headstrong lunkhead I am used to?"

"We came up here to make a baby," Zach reminded her. "Not to put our lives at risk."

"This from the man who once wanted to take on the entire Piegan tribe single-handed?"

"I was young and I was mad," Zach said.

"Really, I am fine with going on." Lou started up the bank. "The glacier isn't that far off. If we push, we can reach it before the sun goes down and set up camp."

"I am not fine with it."

Lou stopped and half turned. "You're serious? You would give up when we are over halfway there?"

"Is it that you don't want to make a baby?" Zach rejoined.

"What are you talking about?" Lou asked. "Coming up here was my idea, remember?"

"Then we should do what we came up here to do and not let your curiosity be the death of us."

Her brow knitting, Lou came back down. "What's gotten into you? You never talk about death or dying."

Zach came over and lightly kissed her on the brow. "I have been doing a lot of thinking. About how much you mean to me. About what my life would be like without you."

"Oh."

"The thing at the glacier has not bothered us the whole time we have been in the valley. Why should we bother it? Let's leave well enough alone, and if we are going to start our family, then let's by God get started."

Lou gazed at the distant bulk of ice and snow, then into her husband's evergreen eyes. "You've convinced me. That last meadow we passed is as likely a spot as any to set up camp." She giggled. "Although we might not live long enough to reach it."

"What are you talking about?"

"Zachary King, the voice of reason?" Lou glanced at the sky and then at the ground and then all around them. "The world should come to an end any second now."

Zach laughed and embraced her and their lips met. "You are a hopeless tease, do you know that?"

"It's just one of the many sterling qualities you adore about me," Lou said.

"I had forgotten how humble you are," Zach retorted, and kissed her again. Laughing, he turned her around and swatted her on her bottom. "Let's get to that meadow while you have me in the mood."

Lou batted her eyelashes at him. "The mood for what, kind sir?"

"Making babies."

"Did you bring a picnic basket?"

That gave Zach pause. "A what?"

"When I was little, one day I asked my father where babies come from," Louisa related. "He told me the stork brings them in a picnic basket.

As ungainly as you are, you are sure not a stork. And I don't see a picnic basket."

Grinning, Zach gave her another playful swat. "Picnic baskets are how they did it in the old days. They have invented a new way that is a lot more fun."

Lou's eyelashes underwent another flurry. "What way would that be, handsome stranger?"

Zach threw back his head and roared. "Egads, woman. Or should I call you wench?"

"Egads?" Louisa repeated. "You have been hanging around Shakespeare too long. And you may call me whatever you like so long as you leap to do my bidding."

Their spirits high, they climbed on their mounts and headed back down the mountain to the sunlit meadow with its gentle waving grass and colorful patchwork of wildflowers.

High above, deep in its dark and frigid lair, the Thing in the glacier stirred. Growling, it rose and shuffled to the opening but was careful to stand well back so its silhouette was not outlined against the ice.

The Thing was restless. It could not say why, but it had been restless for some time. It did not sleep soundly. It could not lie still for days at a time doing nothing. It felt a newfound urge to roam, to prowl, to release the impulse in physical activity.

But the Thing did not like the daytime. It did not like the sun. It had dwelled in the dark for so long that the light hurt its eyes.

Squinting, the Thing edged outward, and

sniffed. Its sense of smell, like all its senses, was exceptionally keen. So it was that the movement far below was immediately noticed.

A snarl escaped its throat as the Thing hunched forward, its glittering eyes slits against the bright glare. It stared until its eyes watered, with an unholy intensity that did not bode well for whatever had attracted its interest.

Far down the mountain two riders appeared. They were so far off they were little more than stick figures, but the Thing knew them for what they were. They entered the forest and were lost to view.

The Thing dropped flat and crawled to the edge of the overlook. After that it did not move, not so much as a muscle, as the sun slowly climbed the vault of sky and started on its long descent. The Thing might as well have been carved from the ice for all the life it showed. Only its eyes betrayed it. Only those glittering eyes, with their bestial vitality.

Eventually the Thing's patience was rewarded.

The riders reappeared lower down, in a meadow. They stopped and dismounted.

Another snarl filled the lair. The creature rose slightly, every nerve aquiver. Even at that distance he saw that the pair were moving about doing things that suggested to its mind they intended to stay for the night.

All of a sudden, the Thing spun and retreated into the dark depths of its den. It crouched, placed its forehead on the ice, and whined. It clawed at the ice, the whine becoming a growl, the growl becoming a snarl, the snarl rising to a roar that seemed to shake the ice walls.

The Thing fell silent. It did not move. But it was not sleeping. It crouched with its eyes open, staring at nothing, an occasional scratch of its claws the only sign it was alive, as the light in its lair faded to gray and then to black. Even then the Thing did not rouse.

More time passed.

Finally the Thing rose and moved to the opening. It rose to its full height and stood sniffing the air. A vast black gulf stretched below. A sea of emptiness mantled in night. Only eyes as keen as the Thing's could discern the shapes of trees and boulders.

In all that great ocean of black was a solitary splash of color, fingers of red and orange that licked at the dark.

From lower down the mountain came the howl of a wolf, and to the north the shriek of the biggest of cats. But the Thing had no interest in them. Not tonight. It was only interested in the fingers of red and orange. It knew what fire was, although it could not say how it knew, just as it could not articulate how it knew what the riders were.

A feral grin creased the Thing's mouth. Its tongue flicked over its sharp teeth. Its stomach rumbled, reminding the Thing how hungry it was.

Savage elation filled its viens, and the Thing opened its mouth to roar its challenge. But the roar was never uttered. Abruptly, it lowered itself over the edge of the ice cliff.

There was no moon, but the Thing moved surefootedly down the face of the glacier and into the trees. Here it stopped to again test the wind, and listen. As silent as the stars above, it moved to where the stream flowed out from under the glacier and off down the mountain. Squatting, it drank its full of the deliciously cold water.

In a crouch, the Thing followed the stream. It went slowly, for it was not the only predator abroad. Twice it spooked deer that bounded off in fear, but it did not give chase. Not this night. Tonight the Thing was only interested in the beings that had made the fire.

Eventually the Thing came to where a gravel bar jutted from the bank and drew up in midstride to noisily sniff and turn this way and that. Its movements became almost frantic as it lowered its nose to the ground and bounded down the bank to the bar. It sniffed at a large set of prints and then at a small set, and then stood stock-still, sniffing the small set again and again.

The night was host to a new sound, a whine such as a puppy might make. The Thing scurried back up the bank and turned in the direction the scent led him, down the mountain toward the distant meadow.

A new eagerness animated the Thing. Every so often it whined. It stopped whining when it came to the edge of the forest that fringed the meadow. It did not venture into the open. It crouched and stared at the creatures by the fire. The smaller of the pair interested it most.

The Thing yearned to get closer. It circled the meadow, seeking in vain for a way to reach the pair without being seen. But the ring of light cast by the fire reached almost to the trees.

Suddenly the Thing stopped. In its preoccupation with the small creature, it had forgotten about their mounts. A whinny reminded him. One of the animals had raised its head and pricked its ears.

The pair by the fire stood. They had long sticks in their hands. Strange sticks unlike any the Thing ever saw. A sense of unease came over it. The Thing smothered a growl.

The larger of the pair—the male—bent and reached into the fire. Or so it appeared. When it straightened it held a thick branch, one end of which glowed red with flames. Holding the brand aloft, the male strode to the animals. He stared toward the forest—stared directly at the spot where the Thing was crouched.

The smaller of the pair—the female—made sounds. The male responded, then slowly advanced. Both the male and the female pressed the long sticks to their shoulders.

The Thing's unease grew. It did not like the fire, did not like the light, did not like that the pair suspected it was there. It started to rise with the intent of hurling itself at them, but instinct took over. Staying low to the ground, it slunk from the approaching light.

The male was wary. Twice he stopped and peered intently into the undergrowth. He came halfway to the trees but stopped when the female made more sounds. He made some, she made more, and the male turned and went back to her.

The Thing could not take its eyes off the female. A hunger that had nothing to do with food caused a gnawing ache deep in the pit of its being.

In time the female lay down to sleep. The male made as if he would sleep, too, but after a while, when light snores came from the female, the male sat back up, added broken branches to the fire, and sat cross-legged with his long stick cradled in his lap. Clearly the male was not going to sleep any time soon.

The breeze brought the scent of a doe. The Thing did not want to leave, but the hunger in its belly eclipsed the gnawing hunger deep within. The Thing faded into the night. It would hunt, and feast, and then maybe return to watch the pair in the hope the male would sleep. A swift rush, and the male would be dead.

And the Thing would have the female.

Chapter Six

Lou was having a marvelous dream. In it, she and Zach had not one, not two, but three children, three bubbling founts of joy and playfulness, and their family was as happy as any had ever been or would be. Two girls and a boy, with the boy in the middle, and all three handfuls. They kept Lou on her toes with their antics. But they were good kids, sweet kids, and they adored her as deeply as she adored them. They would go on walks around the lake. Zach would take them fishing and hunting. If they were going to live in the wilderness, and Lou could not see her husband living anywhere else, they must learn to live off the land. They must learn not only how to survive but how to live comfortably so that their existence was not hand to mouth.

The Shoshones were examples of both.

The eastern Shoshones, or the Snakes as whites usually called them, lived much as the Crows

and the Sioux and the Cheyennes. They depended heavily on the buffalo for food, for hides
for their lodges, and for much else. They owned
many horses. The doeskin dresses of the women
and the buckskin shirts and leggings of the warriors were well crafted. All in all, the Snakes lived
comfortably.

Contrast them with the western Shoshones, or,
as they were more commonly called, the Diggers.
The Diggers wore little in the way of clothes, and
a large part of their diet consisted of roots they
dug out with sticks, hence their name. Instead of
buffalo-hide lodges they lived in brush-and-stick
dwellings scarcely sturdier than paper. They
were a poor tribe, one of the very poorest, their
daily lives an unceasing toil of hand to mouth.

Lou did not want her family to stoop to that
level. Which was why her dream pleased her,
with its sumptuous meals and her children nicely
dressed and their cabin warm and cozy.

Then came the harsh squawk of a jay, and Lou's
dream dissolved in shards, replaced by the bright
glare of the morning sun. She blinked, then rolled
onto her back and stretched. It was a few seconds
before she remembered where she was: a meadow
high on the mountain to the northwest of the
lake. She was surprised Zach had let her sleep so
late. Normally he was up at the break of day.

With a start, Louisa remembered the nervous
behavior of their horses the night before and how
Zach had been sure something was spying on
them from the woods.

Lou glanced to her left, where Zach had spread
his blankets the night before. He was not under

them. They were smooth and flat, and plainly had not been used. Alarm spiked through her. Sitting up, she glanced anxiously about, smiling when she beheld the apple of her eye seated by the fire, his Hawken in his lap, his chin on his chest, asleep. She was about to tease him when she realized he must have stayed up all night without telling her he was going to.

Warmth filled Lou. She loved that man, loved him with all her soul and all her heart. He could be pigheaded—Lord, could he be pigheaded!—and he could be stubborn—Lord, could he be stubborn!—but he was as devoted to her as any woman had any right to expect her man to be, and she did not regret taking him for her husband.

Throwing off the blanket, Lou sat up. She was set to call to Zach and wake him when she thought how nice it would be to fix breakfast first and start his day with a hot meal. Accordingly, she quietly got up, took the coffeepot, and made for the stream. It flowed along the north boundary of the meadow, just inside the trees.

Lou smiled as she walked. She had looked forward to getting away for so long. Zach was not one for what he termed "wastes of time," which seemed to be just about anything that had an element of romance. Time and again she had to drag him up into the high country for a day or three of just the two of them, but those times had been few and far between since they had moved to the new valley. There had been too much to do: building their cabins, chopping a store of wood for the winter, drying and salting enough deer and elk meat to last until the snow melted.

Lou was only a few yards from the forest when it occurred to her that she was about where the lurker in the woods had been the night before. She stopped, troubled by sudden dread. The bright sun and the tranquil woods reassured her. Surely, she told herself, whatever had been there was long gone. She took another step and looked down at herself.

Her carelessness appalled her. She had forgotten to bring her Hawken and her pistols. All she had was her belt knife.

Lou was glad Nate and Winona were not there to see her. They would take her to task, Nate in particular. He was always going on about how all it took was a single mistake to turn a person into worm food. She never much liked that term, worm food. It implied human beings were no more than fodder for nature's scavengers.

Lou scanned the undergrowth. She could hear the stream, but a thicket blocked it from sight. About to turn back for her guns, she squared her slender shoulders and entered the woods. To be scared was silly. Zach was within earshot and would come on the run if she shouted for help.

Amused by her worries, Lou skirted the thicket. A shallow pool spread before her. She had visited it the evening before when they filled the coffeepot. Now she stepped to the same spot, knelt, and dipped the pot in the stream. The cold water sent goose bumps up her arm and down her back. She shivered, then glanced down.

The world receded around her. The chorus of songbirds faded. Lou heard only the pounding of her heart and saw only the tracks that had not been there the evening before, the same sort of tracks they had found at the gravel bar: huge, mishappen, yet human in outline. The claws had sunk inches deep where the thing crouched. Four claws, she counted, the middle claw longer than the rest. They were suggestive of a bear, but no bear ever made tracks like these.

Suddenly Lou heard the birds and the wind and felt the warmth of the sun on her face. It reminded her that she was alone and unarmed and in the same woods as something that had apparently come down from the glacier to stalk them in the dead of night. Another shiver ran through her, but this one had nothing to do with the cold water.

Lou stood and started to back away from the stream. Too late, she sensed a presence behind her. She started to open her mouth to shout for Zach when her shoulder was gripped and she was spun halfway around.

"Are you trying to get yourself killed?"

A constriction in her throat prevented Lou from replying.

"What's the matter? Cat got your tongue?" Zach thrust her rifle at her. "I should think you would know better."

Instead of taking the Hawken, Lou threw her arms around him and hugged him close. "Good morning, handsome," she said huskily.

"Don't try to weasel out by acting nice," Zach said sternly. "If my parents and I have told you once, we have told you a thousand times—"

"Never go anywhere without my guns," Lou finished for him.

"I'm not being mean," Zach said. "I don't want anything to happen to you. When I woke up and saw you were gone and your rifle and pistols lying there, I about laid an egg."

Lou chortled. "So long as you lay a golden egg like that goose."

Zach surveyed the forest. "Well, no harm done, I reckon. But I still ought to take you over my knee and spank you."

"Ha. You've never laid a hand on me." Lou was trying to act lighthearted, but she had to let him know. "There is something you should see." Turning, she pointed.

Zach was past her in a stride and squatted to examine the tracks. "Damn. I knew it. I just knew it."

"I wish you wouldn't swear," Lou said. She never swore. Her father had never cussed, at least not when he was around her, which was nearly all the time after the death of her mother.

"It was watching us," Zach said. "It watched us for a good long while."

"It's gone now," Lou said.

Rising, Zach stared thoughtfully up at the glacier. "Maybe it only comes out at night. That's the only time we ever hear it."

"Some animals are more active at night than during the day," Lou mentioned.

"Mostly the meat-eaters." Zach indicated the tracks. "This settles it. We are packing up and heading down, and I don't want to hear a word to the contrary." He headed for their camp.

Falling into step beside him, Lou took two strides for every one of his. "You're going to hear some whether you want to or not. I had my heart set on this, and I refuse to let a few tracks spoil it."

"You saw those prints. You saw how big they are. You saw the claws. Do you really want to tangle with whatever made them?"

"It didn't attack us last night, did it?" Lou said.

"Maybe it was scared of the fire," Zach argued. A lot of beasts were. Even grizzlies were shy of fire.

"Then it won't bother us so long as we keep a fire going at night," Lou said.

Zach stopped and faced her. "No, you don't. You are not going to change my mind."

"Don't I have a say?" Louisa countered. "You do realize how important this is to me, don't you?"

"Yes," Zach conceded. "But we can't have a baby if we're dead."

"Someone is overreacting. We have our rifles and pistols, and we are not babes in the woods."

Zach's temper flared but he held it in check. "Someone is not thinking clearly. Sure, we have weapons, but does that mean we go out looking for trouble, does it?"

"I can't believe what I'm hearing," Lou said. "Since when have you become the voice of caution?"

Simmering, Zach strode to the fire. Lou snagged at his sleeve, but he continued walking.

"I'm sorry, hon," Lou said when he finally stopped and picked up the coffeepot. "That was uncalled for. But you must admit that you have a history of rash behavior."

Zach stared at her.

"Don't look at me like that. You know you do.

You jump into trouble feet first and worry about the consequences later—if you worry about them at all."

Sighing, Zach sat and patted the ground beside him. After Lou sank down, he filled her tin cup with coffee and handed it o her. Taking a sip of his own, he said, "I won't deny that when I was younger I was a hothead. And yes, before you say anything, I suppose I still am, to a degree."

Lou went to speak, but Zach held up a hand. "Hear me out. Before I met you, my goal in life, as my pa might say, was to be the most famous Shoshone warrior who ever lived. To do that I had to count coup. A lot of coup. More than anyone else. So, yes, I was in my share of scrapes."

"You have been in more than a few since we met," Lou noted.

"Not since my sister was kidnapped," Zach said. "I've made it a point to stay by your side and not go traipsing off looking for enemies to slay."

That was true, and Lou allowed as much, adding, "So you're saying that you have changed your ways?"

"Do any of us ever really change?" Zach wondered. "I'm not much different now than I was when I was ten. I'm older and bigger, but I still like to do the same things I did back then."

"Now you are confusing me," Lou said. "Have you changed or have you not?"

"I wouldn't mind counting more coup. I wouldn't mind going on raids with the Shoshones. But I don't, because of you." Zach clasped her hand. "I love you too much to put you through the worry."

"I thank you for that," Lou said. "But none of this explains why you want to tuck tail and run from whatever made those tracks."

"Do you remember that griz my father killed? The one that chased me and drove me over a cliff?"

"You nearly died."

Zach nodded. "Exactly. It got me to thinking. When we're young we tend to think we are invincible, but we're not."

Louisa grinned. "You're not ready to be put out to pasture yet."

"Quit quibbling. I'm serious, damn it."

"I asked you not to swear."

"And I am asking you to help me pack up and go back down. Not all the way. Say, within half a mile of our cabin. It's far enough that we should be safe." Zach had never seen sign of the creature that far down. Ideally, he would like to get his father and Shakespeare and hunt it, but that could wait until after.

Lou gazed into her cup and swirled her coffee. "That would be all right. I only wanted to come up here in the first place because you were always saying how you'd like to see the glacier up close one day." She smiled and leaned over and kissed him on the cheek. "Just so we have some time alone. I don't much care where. The important thing is to start our family."

"We're agreed, then."

In less than half an hour they were under way. Zach deliberately hung back so that Lou went first and he came after, leading the packhorse.

They rode all day. The descent was a lot easier

than the climb up had been, and they only stopped once to rest the horses. Lou wanted to cook a meal at midday, but Zach told her he was not hungry and would rather wait until evening to eat. Fortunately she did not hear his belly growl all afternoon.

Twilight found them in a clearing in a tract of firs not far from the stream. Zach wanted to push on to the next meadow, but Lou said she was sore from so much time in the saddle and needed to stop. Against his better judgment, Zach gave in.

In due course the sun relinquished its aerial reign and the stars blossomed like so many sparkling flowers, filling the firmament with their multitude. There was no moon.

Lou cooked. Zach sat with his rifle by his leg and one hand on a pistol, listening to the sounds spawned out of the black veil of night and hoping they had descended far enough that the creature would not come after them.

Deep down, he doubted it.

Chapter Seven

The Thing roused early. It had not slept well. It could not stop thinking of the female, of her scent. It tossed and turned and grew hot and itchy. Several times it got up and paced.

The sun was still high in the sky when the Thing rose and padded to the lair entrance. It did not step into the sunlight but rested with its chin on its forelimbs and gazed off down the mountain at the meadow. Suddenly its head snapped up. The female and the male and the animals they rode were not there.

The Thing rose and took several quick steps. The instant sunlight struck it, the Thing recoiled back into the dark. From its throat rose a growl of frustration.

Anxiously, the Thing waited, its gazed fixed on the meadow. Every so often it would sniff and growl.

At length the sun dipped to the horizon. Bit by

bit it was devoured, until only a crescent morsel remained. That, too, was swallowed, and the next instant, the Thing was out of its lair and hastening to the stream. It did not stop to voice its challenge as it was wont to do. In grim silence it flew on the wings of a need it could not define and could not deny. In its urgent need it glanced neither to the right nor the left but hurtled on through the growing dark with tireless vigor.

The meadow lay quiet and still. This time the Thing did not stop at the edge of the trees. It bounded to the middle, to the charred remains of the fire. Squatting, the Thing sniffed and poked. The acrid scent tingled its nose. Turning, the Thing lowered its nose to the ground and sniffed in ever wider circles. Soon it had established which direction its quarry had taken. The tracks of their mounts confirmed his nose.

The Thing started after them. It moved at a steady jog, a pace it could sustain for half a day if need be.

A rabbit in its path was startled into flight. A doe and a fawn panicked at the Thing's scent and fled. Roosting birds took wing.

The Thing was oblivious of the fear it spawned. It cared only about the tracks and the scent.

The night pulsed with sounds. A cougar screeched somewhere to the southwest. To the north a bear roared. Wolves were on the prowl, and as always there were coyotes.

None gave the Thing pause. Coyotes and wolves were no threat; they invariably ran at the Thing's approach. Mountain lions, too, never came near. Perhaps it was his size. Or perhaps it was his strangeness.

Only bears ever dared stand up to him, and even they, when he rushed at them roaring and shrieking and flailing his claws, took flight.

The Thing did not like having its domain invaded. The male who had intruded would find that out.

The female was a different matter.

A very different matter indeed.

Nate King had always loved to read. He had begun the habit at an early age. When he played as a child, he often acted out the parts of characters in the books. At ten he was a Greek warrior in the army that sacked venerable Troy. At eleven he was a gallant knight in armor fighting for a maiden's honor. He made a slingshot and toppled Goliath as David. His father had thought it nonsense; his mother had smiled in her caring manner as he crept through the house with a yardstick to his shoulder in imitation of Daniel Boone.

Nate still loved to read. A particular favorite was James Fenimore Cooper. Critics claimed Cooper's stories were too romanticized, but to Nate, who adored his wife as he adored life itself, romance was part and parcel of existence. Others nitpicked that Cooper belittled the red man, presenting Indians as dull and vulgar, but it was patently untrue. Some of Cooper's Indians were as vivid as real life. Chingachgook, the Deerslayer's friend for many a year; noble, heroic Uncas; cunning, vicious Magua. In Cooper's tales there were good and bad Indians just as there were good and bad whites, and smart and not-so-smart Indians, as there were smart and not-so-smart whites.

Nate was seated in the rocking chair in front of the fireplace, engrossed in *The Deerslayer*, when his wife came in.

"The door to the chicken coop is closed," Winona confirmed. "If that fox comes around it will be disappointed."

Without looking up from his book, Nate remarked, "Sometimes I think those chickens are more bother than they are worth."

"I don't hear you complain when you're stuffing yourself with eggs or when we have roast chicken. But if you want, we can give them away. I'm sure Shakespeare or Zach would be more than happy to take them off our hands."

Nate lowered the book and straightened. "I wasn't saying we should get rid of them. I just said they are a bother."

Winona showed her even white teeth. "That is just as well. You are a bother sometimes, but I would not give you away, either."

Chuckling, Nate let his gaze rove from her resplendent raven hair to her beaded moccasins. For a woman who had been married for two decades and bore two children, she was remarkably fit, her hips not much wider than they had been when they met.

Nate loved her dearly. She was the best helpmate a man could ask for. That she had stuck with him for so long was a never ending source of wonder. She could have had her pick of any Shoshone warrior she took a fancy to, but she had chosen him, a white man. Sure, her people were about the friendliest tribe west of the Mississippi, but she was only the second Shoshone woman ever to marry a white man.

"A slice of apple pie for your thoughts, husband," Winona said. She had made the pie that morning.

"I was thinking of how lucky I am that you care for me," Nate confessed.

"Yes, you are lucky," Winona agreed, her English flawless. A natural-born linguist, she spoke English much better than he spoke Shoshone.

"That is one of the traits that drew me to you," Nate said. "How humble you are."

Winona laughed. "The trait that drew me most to you is your simple nature."

Nate was genuinely shocked. "Did you just call me a simpleton?"

Again her merry laugh filled the cabin. "No. What I admire most is that you do not put on airs. You do not pretend to be someone you are not. You are a simple man."

"Thank you. I think."

Winona opened a drawer and took out a carving knife. "It is a compliment, husband. Many men and women pretend to be that which they are not. They do not see themselves as they truly are but as they would like to be. You are always you."

"Who else would I be?"

Winona lifted the pie from the counter and carried it to the table. "How big a slice would you like?"

"Half should do me."

"Half the pie? What are you trying to do? Put on so much weight I must make you new buckskins?"

"That will be—" Nate began, and stopped, struck by how she had thrown up her head and cocked it toward the window. "What is it? What do you hear?"

Winona did not answer. She hurried to the door, worked the bolt, and flung it open. "Come and listen."

Nate did not need the urging. He was already out of the rocking chair. Still holding *The Deerslayer*, he stepped out into the brisk night air. "I don't hear anything."

"Wait," Winona said, her face raised to the benighted peaks to the northwest. "Maybe it will do it again."

"Do what?"

An answer came in the form of a wavering howl unlike any ever made by a wolf or coyote.

"Strange," Winona said. "Usually we only hear it when the moon is out, but there is no moon tonight."

"I wish Zach and Lou had not gone up there," Nate said. He had more to say, but just then a large bulk loomed around the corner of their cabin and bore down on them.

Zach and Louisa were huddled by the fire, his arm over her shoulder.

They had enjoyed a fine meal. Zach had shot a squirrel shortly before the sun went down and Lou skinned it, chopped the meat into chunks, and dropped the chunks in the pot, along with wild onions, cut green beans they had brought along, and flour. The result was a tasty stew rich with delicious broth. Zach had washed his meal down with coffee, Lou with water, and now they were savoring the quiet of the early night.

"This is nice," Lou commented.

Zach drowsily nodded. He had been up most of the night and needed six or seven hours of solid sleep. But the gleam in his wife's eyes told him he might not get it.

"You don't regret coming up here with me, do you?"

Zach stalled by refilling his tin cup with steaming coffee. If he answered yes, he would be in the doghouse until the cows came home, and they did not own any cows. "That is the silliest question you have ever asked me."

"But do you?" Lou persisted. "I don't want to force a baby on you."

"Have you ever known me to do anything I don't want to?"

"The old Zach, no. But the new Zach has me scratching my head." Lou lightly pressed her lips to his. "Not that I don't appreciate your concern for my well-being."

I should hope to blazes you do, Zach was about to tease her, when the peaceful night was shattered by a howl such as few human ears ever heard. Instantly he was on his feet with a pistol in each hand.

Lou was a shade slower. Unlimbering her flintlocks, she exclaimed, "It's here! It followed us down!"

Zach mentally cursed himself for making camp in the clearing. They were surrounded by tall firs, rank after rank of tightly spaced trunks. The howl had seemed to come from their right, but the creature could be anywhere.

"What do we do?" Lou whispered. She peered into the firs until her eyes hurt, but all she saw was black. "We can't stay here in the open like this."

Zach disagreed. "That is exactly what we should do. If it rushes us, we'll see it."

All three horses began nickering and prancing. Nostrils flaring, they stared at the south edge of the clearing.

"It's there," Zach said, gesturing with a pistol. Thumbing back the hammer, he took a step, only to have his arm gripped.

"Where do you think you're going?"

"I might spot it."

"Not on your life," Lou urged. "We stick together. Let it come to us, like you said."

Zach's every instinct was to go after the thing, but common sense prevailed. Animals could see better in the dark. If the beast jumped him, he might need to resort to his bowie. Bowies were formidable, but at close quarters so were fangs and claws.

A twig snapped to their left.

Was the creature circling them? Zach wondered. "Let's stand back to back," he directed. "You watch that side, and I'll watch this side."

Lou was quick to comply. She felt her shoulder blades brush him and pressed closer, deriving strength from the contact. The night had gone quiet again. The wildlife seemed to be holding its collective breath. "What do you think?" she whispered.

"That you should hush." Zach was listening for the stealthy tread of bestial paws but heard only the breeze. Suddenly bending, he grabbed a burning brand from the fire.

"What are you doing?"

"Watch my back," Zach said, and ran at the firs to their left, holding the torch on high. He thought he saw something dart away from the light, but he couldn't be sure. The temptation to give chase was almost overpowering.

"Get back here!" Lou cried. She had as much grit as the next woman, but she would be darned if she would let him leave her there alone.

Zach backpedaled, the torch in front of him in case the creature attacked. But it was wily, their stalker. The creature did not come after him.

"I have an idea," Lou said.

"Let me hear it." Zach was open to any brainstorm that would keep their hides intact.

"We set the woods on fire."

Zach glanced at her. "Sure. As dry as everything is, we can burn down the entire valley while we're at it."

"No. Just these trees," Lou said, with a bob of her chin at the firs. "It should drive the thing off."

"We can't control a fire that big." To Zach the notion was preposterous. "And we don't want to drive it off. We want to lure it in so we can kill it."

"We do?"

The packhorse suddenly whinnied and rose onto its hind legs. As it came back down a front hoof struck the wooden picket pin, which broke with a loud *crack*. Another moment, and the pack-horse bolted into the firs.

Zach lunged in a vain bid to stop the animal from fleeing, but he missed and had to watch in helpless vexation as the horse vanished in the gloom.

It did not get far. There came a sound, a loud thud, as if the horse had collided with a tree. Then there was the crash of underbrush and a strident whinny cut short by another thud.

The two remaining horses were shaking with fear.

Lou flicked her tongue over her dry lips but had no spit with which to moisten them. To the south, a dark shadow darted between trees. She spun, taking swift aim. But the shadow was gone before she could shoot. "What *is* it? A bear?"

Zach was wondering the same thing. It distracted him when he could ill afford to let his attention lapse, a mistake that proved costly.

"Look out!" Lou screamed, pointing.

Zach glanced up.

Chapter Eight

Zach's reflexes had been honed on the whetstone of necessity. He had lived in the wilds his whole life. On countless occasions, whether he lived or died had depended on how quickly he reacted.

But this time Zach was a shade too slow. He glanced up, saw what was arcing toward him, and started to dive to his right, knowing in the split instant he moved that he would not leap clear in time. The melon-sized rock would crush his skull like an eggshell. But even as she shouted, Lou shoved him with all her might.

Zach came down on his hands and knees. There was a thud behind him. He turned, about to break into a smile and thank Lou for saving him. The smile died.

Louisa was on her side, her eyes closed, the rock next to her, a large gash above her ear streaming blood.

For a span of heartbeats Zach was paralyzed

with horror. Then he was on his feet, his blood roaring in his veins. "Lou?" he yelled. A short step, and he was on one knee, reaching for her to cradle her in his lap.

The crack of a twig warned him.

Zach looked up and beheld a large dark something bounding through the firs toward them. The thing growled as it charged, its forelimbs windmilling, claws glinting dully in the glow from the fire. He could not see it clearly, but he did not need to. He pointed at the center of the bulk, steadied his arm, and fired.

At the blast, the creature lurched to a stop. It looked down at itself and roared. Then it was gone, vanishing abruptly and silently. One moment it was there; the next it wasn't. The crash of underbrush testified to its flight.

Zach set both pistols down and tenderly slid a hand under Lou's head. He examined the wound while feeling for a pulse. Her heartbeat was strong and regular. He carefully lifted her, moved closer to the fire, and sank down next to the full water skin they always kept handy. He tenderly placed Lou across his legs. He opened the water skin and applied the cool liquid to Lou's gash. Then he cupped more water and slowly let it trickle between her parted lips.

Groaning and coughing, Lou blinked her eyes and gazed about in confusion. "Where—" she began, and abruptly sat up, or tried to. Clutching her head, she sagged against his chest and groaned.

"Stay still," Zach said.

"The animal?" Lou weakly asked.

"I shot it, and it ran off." Only then did it hit Zach. He stared at the rock smeared red with his wife's blood. "I'm not so sure it *is* an animal."

Lou swallowed, her gaze swiveling up to him. "What do you mean?"

"Animals don't throw rocks."

"It can't be human," Lou said. "You saw the tracks. They are more like those of a bear than a person."

"Don't talk," Zach said. She was ungodly pale. It occurred to him that there might be internal damage. Fear flashed through him, raw, potent, nearly immobilizing fear. If she were to die— He could not finish the thought.

Moving slowly so as not to jar her, Zach placed her on her back on a blanket and pulled a saddle over for a pillow. She started to prop herself up on her elbows, and he quickly slid his arm under her shoulders.

"Let me."

"Thank you." Lou was becoming more alert. She scanned the firs and said, "Are we safe? Is that thing still out there?"

Zach placed her pistols in her hands. "If you see it, give a holler." Hurriedly, he opened a parfleche and took out a small pouch that contained medicines prepared by his mother. They never went up into the mountains without it, not after the incident with the wolverine.

Few whites were aware that Indians had remedies for practically every ill under the sun. Dogwood bark was boiled in water and the tea used to strengthen the heart and as a general tonic. Clematis was used to treat fever. Juniper berries were good for the kidneys. Elderberry helped reduce inflammation. In this instance, after dabbing at the gash with a cloth until the bleeding nearly stopped, Zach applied a plantain poultice. To protect the wound from dirt and possible infection, he cut a strip from a blanket and wound it around her head, tying a knot to hold it in place.

"Thank you," Lou said when he was done.

"It will have to do until I can get you to my mother."

"I'm fine," Lou said.

"Fibber." Zach reclaimed his flintlocks and reloaded the one he had fired. He wedged them under his belt. Placing both rifles next to Louisa, he said, "I must go over to the horses. Watch my back."

Gripping a pistol in each hand, Lou went to rise.

"No." Zach put a hand on her shoulder. "From where you are." He did not want her to move about. It could set her wound to bleeding again.

Lou twisted as he moved away from her, saying, "They look fine to me."

"I'll only be a minute."

The horses were only twenty feet away, but it seemed a lot farther. Zach's main concern was the picket pins. With all the rearing and stamping the horses had done, the pins might come loose. They had already lost one horse; he preferred not to lose another.

It was good he checked. The picket pin Lou's mount was tied to was secure, but the one to his own was half out. He pounded it back in, gave each rope a tug, then returned to his wife.

"I'm fit to ride if you want to leave," Lou said.

"Daybreak we'll head out," Zach told her. To do so in the dark invited disaster. He scooped up his Hawken. "You try and get some rest. I'll wake you when the sun comes up."

"I can help keep watch," Lou offered. "You haven't had much sleep the past few days."

"I'm not the one wearing a turban," Zach joked.

"If you're not sleeping, I'm not sleeping."

Lou tried. She really tried. But bit by bit her eyelids drooped and her chin fell to her chest. She struggled to raise her head, but the demands of exhaustion and her wound would not be denied.

Zach was glad she had succumbed. She needed the rest. Rising, he made a circuit of the clearing, probing the firs for telltale sign of the creature. But there was none. Either it was biding its time and cannily lying low until it could jump them, or it had gone.

Zach did not care to encounter it a third time. As soon as the sun was up, they were heading down the mountain. With Lou in the shape she was in, they could not travel very fast. It would take them an extra day or two to reach their cabin.

Zach hoped he had inflicted a mortal wound. He hoped the thing had crawled off to die and they had seen the last of it. But premonition told him his hope was in vain. Whatever it was, it would come back, probably when they least expected.

He sat down close to Lou. The fire had dwindled, so he added fuel and placed the coffeepot on to boil. There was nothing like scalding hot coffee to help stay awake.

The night was unnaturally quiet. In all that vastness, not so much as a coyote yipped.

Zach looked at Lou. She was so beautiful in repose. So much for starting their family, he reflected. Their high country lark had turned into a trial. He was genuinely worried—not for himself but for Louisa. He kept on staring at her, barely aware when his own eyelids drooped.

The rider brought his pinto to a stop and smiled at Nate and Winona. He clasped his hands together, the back of his left hand to the ground. In sign language it meant "peace." Then he raised his right hand in front of his neck, the first two fingers extended, and brought the tips of the fingers up near his head. In sign talk, it was "friend."

"Neota!" Winona exclaimed in surprise.

The tall warrior swung down. A powerfully built man, he wore buckskins typical of his people. A bow and quiver were slung across his back. At his hip hung a bone-handled hunting knife. His black hair was marked with streaks of gray that had not been there the last time they saw him, and his handsome features bore the stamp of indelible sorrow.

Nate was as surprised as his wife. Neota was a widely respected Ute, high in the councils of his tribe. He was also one of the few Utes who regarded Nate as a friend. In sign language Nate said, "We have plenty food. My heart happy friend here."

There was no sign for "of" or "is," just as there weren't signs for a lot of English words. With a little imagination, though, Nate could mix and match the hundreds of signs he had learned to make himself understood on just about any subject.

Once, years ago, he had asked Winona exactly how many sign gestures there were and been taken aback to find out she did not know. The best she could estimate was eight to nine hundred, although some of her people pegged the total at well over a thousand.

"Question," Winona now signed to their visitor. "To what do we owe this honor?"

This was not exactly what she asked: Nate mentally filled in the blanks. He was curious, too, since their valley was not in Ute country proper, as their former homestead had been.

"I want come many sleeps," Neota signed. "Much sad over Niwot."

Nate understood, partly. Niwot had been Neota's nephew. The young warrior had taken a shine to Nate's daughter, Evelyn, and come courting, Indian fashion, every chance he got. On one of those visits Niwot had been slain by a hostile tribe. Several times since, Neota had shown up, stayed a day or two, and left again without doing much more than walking along the lake. Nate suspected that Neota somehow blamed himself for his nephew's death, but so far Neota had not confided in them.

Neota's hands flowed in sign. "Question. What you do?"

"We listen," Nate signed, and pointed to the northwest, in the direction of the glacier. To his amazement, Neota took a step back, his face reflecting some sort of inner turmoil.

The howling had stopped.

Winona stepped to the doorway and signed for Neota to enter. "You always welcome our lodge."

When Neota, still staring with a stricken look to the northwest, hesitated, Nate motioned and smiled to reassure him. He followed Neota in and went to close the door. He almost had it shut when he thought he heard something and yanked it open again to poke his head out and tilt his ear toward the glacier.

Winona noticed. "What is it, husband?"

Nate drew his head in and shrugged. "I'm not sure. I thought I heard a shot."

Neota was standing by a chair, politely waiting to be invited to sit. It was on his last visit that he tried a chair for the first time. Prior to that he always sat on the floor.

"Please," Nate said in English, pulling the chair out.

Neota unslung his ash bow and quiver of arrows and placed them on the table. His back as rigid as a broom, he slowly sat. He said a few words in Ute.

Winona, always better at languages, remarked, "Something about it being 'the time.'"

"The time for what?" Nate asked, sinking into the chair at the end of the table.

"Let me pour some coffee and we can ask."

Nate was torn between his curiosity over their guest's late arrival and unusual behavior, and a desire to go outside and listen for more sounds from the glacier. He was worried, keenly worried, although he had no real reason to be. They had heard the mysterious howls scores of times and nothing ever came of them. But none of his loved ones had ever gone up to the glacier before.

Neota might as well have been carved from wood for all the life he showed. Unblinking, he stared at the wall. Nate had the impression the warrior's gaze was directed inward.

Winona brought over a tray. On it were three china cups brimming with coffee, the sugar bowl, and three spoons.

Neota did not so much as acknowledge the cup was in front of him, not until Nate reached over and tapped it with his spoon. As if coming out of a daze, Neota shook himself, then carefully slid both hands under the cup and raised it to his mouth. He sipped noisily, smacked his lips, and set the cup down again.

Nate waited for the warrior to sign to them, but when a few minutes had gone by and Neota went on staring at the wall, Nate coughed to get his attention, then asked in sign language, "Question. Why you here?"

"Question. Remember last visit?" Neota signed.

Nate and Winona swapped glances. The last had been about a month ago. They had talked about Niwot, as they always did, about how he had been a fine, upstanding young man, and wasn't it a shame that he had been killed before he could take Nate's daughter for his wife?

Nate glanced over his shoulder at the door to Evelyn's room. She had turned in an hour ago and was no doubt sound asleep. Which was just as well. Neota's visits troubled her, in no small part because she had never intended to marry Niwot, and had been telling him that when Niwot was slain.

Winona signed that yes, she remembered, and that she also remembered telling Neota that the time for tears was long since past and they should get on with their lives.

At that, Neota frowned. "I no forget nephew," he signed. "My fault him die."

"Enemy kill him," Nate signed. The notion that Neota was somehow to blame was preposterous.

"Me," the Ute signed. "I no stop Niwot come. Your valley bad medicine. But I no stop."

Winona signed the question that was uppermost on Nate's mind. "Question. How bad medicine? You never say."

The Ute bowed his head. When after a while he looked up at them, fires burned deep in his dark eyes. "You want know? I tell you."

Chapter Nine

His Ute name was To-Ma.

He was born on a windy winter's day when the sky was bleak with the threat of snow. He was no different from any other Ute boy ever born except that everyone commented on his size. He was a third again as big and heavy as most babies.

From cradleboard to waddling to his first tentative steps, To-Ma had a normal Ute childhood. He was deeply adored by his parents, particularly his mother, who doted over him too much, the father complained.

To-Ma was happy. He ate, he played, he did the few chores he was given to do, and all the while he continued to grow. By seven winters, he was as big as boys who had seen ten or eleven.

Everyone marveled. He would be a mighty warrior, was the common opinion. He would count many coup and heap glory on his people.

Only seven, and some whispered that one day he might be chief of all the Utes.

Then came the following summer. To-Ma's mother took him to pick berries along a river near their village. She did not ask her husband or anyone else to accompany them. The berries were not far. If trouble reared, she would shout, and warriors would flock to her aid.

They each had half a basket full, the boy and his mother, when she, in the lead, stopped so unexpectedly that To-Ma bumped into her. He nearly spilled his basket and let out a squawk. The next moment his mother's hand was over his mouth, and she was hurrying toward their village. She tried to carry him so they could go faster, but although only eight, he weighed almost as much as she did. She had to lower him, and her hand slipped from his mouth.

To-Ma raised a yell of protest at her treatment. Again his mother covered his mouth, and bending, she whispered in his ear, "Be quiet or we are dead."

To-Ma did not know what she was talking about. All he cared about were the berries he had nearly dropped, the sweet, delicious berries he loved to eat. Then he heard a grunt, and gazing past her, saw that which had filled his mother with fear.

It was a bear. A great, gigantic bear the likes of which To-Ma had never imagined existed. Its maw looked big enough to swallow him whole.

"Scar!" his mother gasped, a hand pressed to her throat, and gave To-Ma a shove that caused him to trip and nearly fall. He stayed on his feet, but he dropped his basket and his precious berries spilled over the grass.

"Mother!" To-Ma yelled, about to burst into tears. She had never treated him so roughly. It scared him more than the bear.

"Run!"

To-Ma felt his mother's frantic fingers dig into his back. He was propelled toward the lodges with such force, he stumbled and came down hard on his elbows and shins. "Mother!" he cried, but she did not pick him up and dust him off and say how sorry she was. No, she grabbed his wrist and nearly tore his arm from its socket.

"Run, child! Run!"

To-Ma shouted that he did not want to leave the berries, but if his mother heard she paid no heed. He looked back.

The bear was after them. It had a shuffling gait that caused the hump on its shoulders to rise and fall like the prow of a canoe on a tempest-tossed lake.

"Scar!" his mother cried again, more a wail than a scream.

To-Ma never knew what hit him, whether it was his mother or the bear, but suddenly he was sailing through the air. This time he came down on his head. He exploded with pain, and everything around him faded to the ebony of a starless night.

A strange sound brought To-Ma back to the realm of here and now, a *crunch-crunch-crunch* he could not account for. He opened his eyes and sat up, and all that he was and all that he ever would be turned inside out and upside down.

His mother lay a pebble's toss from where he sat. She was on her back, her arms and legs flung wide, her face turned to the blue vault of sky. Her eyes were open wide, her body oddly slack. The giant bear straddled her, a huge paw on her chest. As To-Ma looked on in uncomprehending horror, the bear bit into his mother's throat and tore away a chunk of flesh and skin. In a single gulp it swallowed the morsel and bent its head for more.

Again the bear's razor teeth sliced deep. This time To-Ma understood. "Mother!" he cried. "Mother! Get up and run!"

The bear's ponderous body shifted toward him. In the distance rose angry shouts and screams, but the bear ignored them. Sliding its paw off To-Ma's mother, it came toward To-Ma.

"I was one of the warriors there that day," Neota said. "I saw what the bear we called Scar did next, and like many, I took it as a good omen."

The bear sniffed at little To-Ma, who shouted at it to leave his mother alone. Then To-Ma did that which astounded the onrushing Utes; he punched the grizzly on the nose.

"I expected Scar to claw the child to pieces," Neota related, Nate mentally filling in the gaps in the sign language. "But the bear did nothing. It just stared at the boy, then turned, sank its teeth into the woman's shoulder, and dragged her into a thicket."

It was Neota who scooped To-Ma into his arms and ran with him to the village. By then every warrior was armed. To-Ma's father, who had just returned from deer hunting, hugged the boy to his chest and thanked the Great Mystery aloud for sparing him.

Spreading out in a skirmish line, the Utes advanced on the thicket, only to find Scar was gone. The bear tormented them for many winters afterward.

That incident was Scar's only link to To-Ma's story.

The seasons passed, one after the other. The Utes moved their village many times.

To-Ma grew until he surpassed not only all the boys his age but all the boys of any age, plus all the men. He was big and he was strong, but he was not all that adept with the bow or the lance or the knife. In battle he relied on his brawn rather than his brain, but there was no denying that he was one of the bravest of them, and great things were expected of him.

Sixteen winters went by.

To-Ma and his father were picked to go on a raid, his father one of a dozen warriors selected who had sons who had yet to count coup.

Off they rode, to wage war on their bitter enemies, the Shoshones.

Neota was one of the warriors. In fact, he had organized the war party so that his own son might distinguish himself.

North they headed, into the heart of Shoshone country. All went well until the fateful day when the scout they had sent ahead raced back to inform them a Shoshone village was over the next ridge.

Dismounting, they crept to the top and beheld more lodges than any of them had ever seen in one place at one time. Unknown to them, they had stumbled on a gathering of all the Snakes. There were hundreds of warriors with their women and children, and thousands of horses.

Some of the Utes were for turning back. They argued that there were too many Shoshones, that to raid the village would reap their own extermination. Others were for waiting until the quiet hour before dawn when few Shoshones would be awake. They would help themselves to as many Shoshone horses as they could run off and kill any Shoshones who tried to stop them.

Neota was torn. He was concerned for his son, just as To-Ma's father was concerned for To-Ma. But here was a chance for the boys to perform deeds that would be told and retold around the evening fires for many winters to come. They voted to go through with the raid.

So it was that the next morning, Neota and To-Ma's fathers were among the first to sneak in among the Shoshone horse herd. At a yell from Neota, the Ute warriors leaped on Shoshone horses and began to drive off others.

But the Shoshones were not fools. They did not leave their horses unguarded. It was the job of Shoshone boys to watch the herds and shout an alarm. Since it was almost dawn, most of the boys were fighting off sleep. They were slow to react, but when the most alert of them yelled that the horses were being stolen, all the boys raised cries, bringing warriors from every lodge.

The Utes did not break and run. It was not yet light, and they felt that if they could get the horses they had stolen over the ridge, they could elude pursuit.

Then a Shoshone boy who had been dozing under a tree ran up and pointed at them, bawling, "Here they are! Here they are!"

To-Ma and his father were closest. At a word from his father, To-Ma let fly with an arrow that pierced the young Shoshone's chest. The boy toppled, and the Utes were on the verge of escaping when a score of Shoshone warriors, fleeter than their fellows, burst out of the dark.

The combat was swift and furious. The Utes killed a few Shoshones. The Shoshones killed a few Utes. Neota saw that the war party was hard pressed and shouted for them to leave the stolen horses, and flee.

To-Ma was being pressed the hardest. His size was to blame. It made him easier to spot. More Shoshones had converged on him than any of the other Utes. But he was holding his own, laying about him with a knife, when Neota's shout caused him to take his eyes off the Shoshones and glance toward Neota. An older, wiser warrior would not have made that mistake.

It was the opening a charging Shoshone needed. Armed with a heavy war club, he sprang high into the air and brought his club crashing down on To-Ma's head. He misjudged his leap and fell against To-Ma's horse, which saved To-Ma's life. For the horse, spooked by the bedlam, and stung by the scrape of the war club, bolted.

The Utes retreated. Once over the ridge, they switched to their own mounts and looped ropes around the necks of the horses they had stolen. Only then did someone notice that To-Ma was still on the Shoshone horse, his large frame bent nearly double. To-Ma's father and Neota discovered that To-Ma was unconscious from a hideous head wound. The back of his skull had splintered, and there was a hole in the bone large enough for a man to stick a fist through. But To-Ma still breathed.

It took seven of them to lift To-Ma and tie him on his own horse. Quickly they mounted and were off. The yells of the Shoshones were uncomfortably near. Any moment, the Utes expected to be overtaken and to have to fight for their lives anew.

They pushed their mounts to the point of collapse. When the animals could not go any farther, they made their stand in a narrow canyon where only a few Shoshones at a time could get at them. They waited, nerves taut, weapons ready, but the Shoshones did not appear.

In the dark the Shoshones had lost them.

It was a grim band that returned to the Ute village. The lament of the women who had lost husbands and sons was terrible to hear. Even so, the raid was accounted a success. They had counted coup on the Shoshones and stolen valuable horses.

None of which was consolation to To-Ma's father. He sat by young To-Ma day and night, tending him. In that, he was aided by several of the more experienced healers.

To-Ma was unconscious for many sleeps. His dressings had to constantly be changed, and he had to be force-fed broth. His great frame became gaunt with hunger. But gradually the shattered bone knit.

To their ministrations To-Ma owed his life. There came a day when his father happened to look over and saw that his son's eyes were open. Elated, he rushed over. His eyes brimming with tears, he asked how To-Ma was feeling.

To-Ma did not reply.

To the father's consternation, To-Ma did not respond to anyone or anything. He just lay there, unblinking, staring at nothing. He would not eat unless helped. For many sleeps the strange state persisted.

Then one morning To-Ma rose of his own accord. He moved about the lodge touching things and making sounds that were not speech but more akin to the guttural grunts of animals. His father tried to talk to him but received no answer. Indeed, at one point To-Ma came up to him and touched him as To-Ma had been touching everything else, as if it were all new to him and he did not know what anything was.

The healers applied all their skill, but in the end it was to no avail.

The father's sorrow was heartbreaking to behold. To-Ma could fend for himself; he would eat when hungry and drink when thirsty, and he attended to his bodily functions. But he behaved atrociously. He loped about the village on all fours. He was always sniffing things and people. Worse, he snarled at the village dogs and growled at anyone who came too close.

A council was held. It was the general opinion that To-Ma's mind had gone, and his spirit taken over by the spirit of an animal. The kind of animal seemed obvious. With his grunts and snarls and shuffling movements, he resembled nothing so much as a bear. Despite the strain to the general harmony, he was permitted to remain in the village.

For a while all went well. The Utes felt sorry for To-Ma's father, and for his sake tolerated the antics of the bear-boy. Until the fateful day when several younger boys teased To-Ma by throwing rocks at him, and To-Ma attacked them. Roaring savagely, he cuffed them with sweeping blows of his huge hands. He scared them more than harmed them, and scared many of the villagers, too.

Another council was held. To-Ma's father was urged to keep a tighter rein on To-Ma.

The father tried. He was devoted to the boy, and to the end he sustained the hope that To-Ma would come to his senses and all would be as it had been.

The end came one summer's eve when the village lay quiet under the blossoming stars.

The father cooked supper and gave To-Ma a slab of roast deer meat. As was To-Ma's wont now that he was a bear, he turned his back and went at the meat as a bear would, ripping and tearing and growling.

The father knew not to go near To-Ma when he was eating. To-Ma would bristle and snarl. But this evening the father forgot, and brought over a handful of blueberries. The father remembered how fond his son had always been of berries of all kinds, and he held them out for To-Ma to see. In reaching down, he brushed the deer meat To-Ma was devouring.

A roar was heard by everyone in the village. Men and women came on the run. Since the flap was down, they did not enter the lodge but called out to To-Ma's father asking if everything was all right. When there was no answer save for the most hideous snapping and rending sounds, the boldest of them peered inside.

To-Ma was crouched over his father. The father's throat had been torn open, and To-Ma was biting off chunks of flesh and lustily chewing.

The Utes waited until To-Ma had gorged himself and was sleeping. Twenty of the huskiest men crept into the lodge, and nearly all were bitten or bruised before they succeeded in binding him.

Yet another council. The unthinkable had occurred. Ute must never kill Ute. The punishment was unavoidable and severe: banishment. Some argued that since To-Ma was now a bear, the taboo did not apply to him. To which others responded that was all the more reason to banish him. As one warrior put it, "We can not have a bear running about our village."

So banishment it was. But some felt to send To-Ma out into the wilderness, unarmed and alone, was the same as killing him. An elder settled the discussion with an idea that appealed to all sides.

The Utes dressed To-Ma in a bear skin complete with claws. He lay strangely docile, never once growling or resisting.

The next decision was where to take him.

It was Neota who had the answer.

Chapter Ten

"You brought him here," Nate King signed.

"Yes," Neota confirmed.

He explained. The valley was far enough away that the Utes doubted To-Ma could find his way back. It had game and water, and so far as they knew, no other tribe claimed it as part of their territory. One other factor recommended it; the valley was bad medicine.

Nate held up a hand, stopping the recital. "Question," he signed. "Valley bad medicine before bring boy?"

That was indeed the case. For as long as any Ute could remember, the valley had been shunned. No Ute would set foot in it.

"Question," Winona signed. "Why bad medicine?"

The story was this: Long ago, when the Utes first came to the mountains, they found a paradise abundant with all they needed. They explored it thoroughly, and one day a party of hunters discovered the hidden valley with its beautiful sparkling lake. When the hunters returned, they told of their find.

Several families immediately set out to construct their lodges along the lakeshore. The rest followed at a leisurely pace. There was talk of the valley becoming their new home.

But when the rest of the Utes arrived, a shocking sight greeted them. The lodges of the three families had been destroyed. The thick buffalo hides had been ripped to ribbons and all their belongings broken to bits or scattered about. Of the families there was no sign.

Quite naturally, the Utes assumed enemies were to blame. The missing people were undoubtedly captives. But when they cast about for sign of the enemy, perplexity set in. For instead of hoofprints and the tracks of moccasin-clad warriors, they found animal tracks, tracks unlike any they had ever seen. Round, the tracks were, and as big as the largest tracks of the largest of their stallions. But these had not been made by hooves. They were paw prints. To some they resembled cat tracks. Others were not so sure.

A small child found the first body. She was frolicking with other children near the forest and came on a trail of dark red drops that fascinated her. She followed the drops, and when she saw the source, she screamed for the first time in her life.

One of the missing warriors had been disemboweled. His intestines had oozed out and lay in thick coils. But what horrified the Utes more was the dead man's expression.

The next body, a woman's, was farther in. She had been clawed apart and one of her arms torn off.

Unease spread. The women and children were hustled back to the lake. Half the warriors stayed to protect them while the other half ventured into the foreboding woods in search of more bodies. They found them, too, every missing person, every man, woman, and child, all as badly mangled, if not worse. The bodies were brought to the lake. It was then that an old warrior noticed something everyone else had overlooked.

None of the bodies had been eaten. Not one showed a trace of bite marks. They had been slain and left to rot. What made it all the more bewildering was that coyotes, vultures, and other scavengers had left the bodies alone. It was unheard of.

That evening, as the Utes huddled around their campfires debating what to do, they heard an eerie cry from high up on the mountains. An awful cry, part roar, part shriek, part howl. It was repeated, again and again throughout the long night.

Few of the Utes could sleep.

It did not take a profound stretch of logic to link the torn bodies with the bestial cries. Whatever was up there had come down and slain them. And there was every chance the creature would come down again.

The next morning the lakeshore was empty. From that day on the valley was considered bad medicine and shunned. Not a single Ute set foot in it until that fateful day when Neota, at the head of two dozen warriors, brought To-Ma there, draped over a horse. Ten of them lowered him to the ground. He snarled and tried to bite them but quieted after they stood back.

Neota, himself, snuck up behind To-Ma and cut the ropes. To-Ma lay there awhile before he realized he was free. With a shrug he cast the ropes off, then rose and bounded on all fours toward the trees. He did not look back. The last they saw of him, he was well up a mountain, rapidly climbing.

The Utes did not linger. Now the valley was bad medicine twice over.

To-Ma was never mentioned again, not at council, at any rate. The subject was as taboo as the valley.

But in the solitude of their lodges, he was sometimes discussed, and many came to think that what they had done was wrong. They had banished someone incapable of understanding why he was being banished. That they had left him in that terrible valley, of all places, compounded their feelings of guilt.

Which explained why none of the Utes came to warn the Kings and the McNairs when it was learned they had moved there. Many Utes, Neota among them, believed To-Ma to be long dead. Neota visited the valley a few times to see how the white men and their families were faring and reported to his people that all was well.

When Niwot decided to court Evelyn King, Neota said nothing. To-Ma's banishment took place nearly thirty winters ago, long before Niwot was born. Niwot had heard the tale, of course, but he was young and in love and would not be put off by talk of bad medicine.

Now, in the silence that fell after Neota stopped speaking, Nate and Winona looked at one another.

"What do you make of it, husband?"

"The Utes did what they had to," Nate said. "Head injuries can do strange things. To-Ma was a danger to them and their children."

"Not him," Winona said. "What do you make of the other thing? The creature that wiped out those three Ute families?"

"It could have been anything," Nate remarked. "A bear, a mountain lion, you name it."

"But Neota said the tracks they found were not those of any animal the Utes knew," Winona reminded him.

Nate shrugged. "Whatever it was, that was thirty years ago."

"*Something* is up there. We heard it earlier. We have heard it many times since we came here. And now our son and his wife are up there with it and their lives might be in danger."

"Which is why I am going up after them," Nate announced, rising.

Winona, too, stood. "I am going with you. He is my son as well as yours."

With a nod at the closed bedroom door, Nate said, "Someone has to stay with Evelyn. If she woke up and found us both gone she would panic. Pack a parfleche for me and I'll go saddle my bay."

"Why must I be the one to stay and not you? I

can ride as well as you. I can shoot almost as well."

"Because you are her mother."

"You are her father."

"Because she is closer to you than she is to me."

"Nonsense."

"Because I am the man, and a man protects those he loves."

"And women do not?"

Exasperated with her, Nate asked, "Why are you making such a fuss? You know it has to be me."

"I do not want you to go alone," Winona said. "Shakespeare and Blue Water Woman can watch Evelyn."

"I'm not going alone. Neota is going with me."

"How do you know? You have not asked him."

To Winona's annoyance, Neota agreed. She filled a parfleche with pemmican, jerky, coffee, and other items and carried it out to the corral. Nate had the bay saddled and was tightening the cinch.

"Why not ride to Shakespeare's and ask him to go along? There is safety in numbers. Is that not what the whites say?"

"It will be a long, hard ride, and he's not as spry as he used to be," Nate responded. He mustered a grin. "Tell him I said that and I'll deny it."

Winona folded her arms across her chest and regarded the Ute. "Why do you suppose he confided in us after all this time?"

"Guilt, maybe," Nate speculated. "Niwot's death hit him hard. He likes Zach and Lou. Maybe he doesn't want anything to happen to them." Nate tied the parfleche on the bay and was ready. Embracing her, he kissed her full on the month. "Take care of yourself."

"You have that backward." Winona dug her nails into his arms. "Come back to me, husband. I am used to you keeping my bed warm at night."

"Hussy," Nate said, and laughed.

Winona did not let go. "I mean it. You are my man. I am your woman. If you die my heart will break."

"Enough of that kind of talk," Nate chided. "I aim to die of old age in my rocking chair." He swung onto the saddle.

Neota was already on the pinto and slapped his legs against it when Nate gigged the bay.

Nate glanced over his shoulder at his wife, an hourglass silhouette in the dark. "I will always love you."

"And I you, husband."

The hoot of an owl woke him.

Zach sat up and yawned. The fire had burnt down to a few embers and was giving off smoke. A faint blush on the eastern horizon promised daylight soon.

He had slept for hours. His lapse appalled him. He was lucky the creature from the glacier had not come back. Rising with his rifle in his hand, he stretched, then pivoted on a heel, surveying the phalanx of firs. His foot bumped the melon-sized rock. Proof the creature had to be a human being. But the notion seemed preposterous. People did not roar, or howl, or act like a beast.

Zach picked up the rock. It was so heavy he had to use both hands. To spare Lou the sight of it—and her blood—when she woke up, he carried the rock a dozen steps and set it down.

Their mounts were still there. He went over and patted them. They were calm, proof the creature must be long gone. He smiled at the thought. He could not stop thinking of it as a *thing*.

Hunkering by the embers, Zach rekindled the fire. The warmth felt good. He broke a limb and added more wood. Lou liked her coffee piping hot in the morning.

Zach glanced at where she lay, and his world came crashing down around him. Unwilling to accept the testimony of his eyes, he groped her blankets, which were flat on the ground.

"Lou?"

Zach jumped up. The natural assumption was that she had gone into the woods.

"Lou?"

He was not worried. Not yet. She had got up before he did and was off doing what most people did. That must be it.

"Lou!"

Zach turned right and left, seeking movement in the vegetation. He cupped his hand to his mouth and sucked in a deep breath.

"Louuuuuuuuuuuuuuuuuuuu!"

His entire body tingling with expectation, Zach waited for her to answer. His shout had spooked a bunch of sparrows into taking wing, but that was all. "Louisa, please," he said softly, and hurled himself at the firs. He plunged in among them, calling her name over and over, calling her name as many times as there were trees, but he received no reply.

Anxiety gnawed at his insides like a thousand ravenous moles. Zach ran back to the clearing. If she were anywhere near, she would come to the clearing.

The horizon was gray, but the sun was not visible. Tapping his foot with impatience, Zach begged, "Come on, come on, come on."

Neither Lou nor the sun acknowledged the request. Gradually the clearing brightened. What he saw sent a wave of fear coursing through him—drag marks, a pair of them, spaced far enough apart that they could have been made by a pair of legs, human legs, the legs of his unconscious wife.

Zach shook his head. "It can't be." Why hadn't he heard anything? Why didn't the creature kill him? Or take him, too? Why only take Lou? A possible answer hit him with the force of a falling tree. He swayed, his head suddenly light, his thoughts scrambled.

The caw of a raven brought Zach out of himself. He saddled his horse faster than he had ever saddled it in his life. He was going to leave Lou's saddle and saddle blanket there, but at the last instant he changed his mind and saddled her horse as well. If he found her she would be grateful.

If. Zach swore at himself. There was no *if.* There was *when. When* he found her. He would find her and spirit her to safety and come back to end the life of whatever took her if he did not end it rescuing her.

"Lou, Lou, Lou," Zach said, a lump in his throat as he climbed into the stirrups.

Lifting the reins, Zach gigged his mount up the

slope. He did not need to track them. He knew where the creature was headed.

As he broke from the firs, a golden arch crowned the sky to the east, heralding the new day.

Zach spied the white mass of the glacier. He also spied a black shape far above. His eyes narrowed as he tried to tell what it was. Given its size, he thought perhaps it was an elk. But it was moving on two legs, not four. He could not be certain due to the distance, but he would swear it had something—or someone—thrown over a shoulder.

"No!" Zach cried, and used his heels to bring his horse to a gallop. "I'm coming, Lou! I'm coming!"

As if the creature heard him, from on high came a mocking howl.

Chapter Eleven

There are degrees of fear.

Louisa King learned that long ago. The fear she felt when a horse threw her when she was ten was nothing like the fear she felt years later when hostiles were out to kill her and her father. That was the worst fear, or so she imagined until the day men showed up at her cabin to kill her husband. She had been so afraid for Zach's life that the fear sapped the vitality from her limbs and the will from her mind. She thought she had plumbed the depths of fear that day, but she was mistaken.

She felt a new depth of fear when she woke up to the sensation of pressure on her mouth. A hairy hand was clamped over it to keep her from crying out. The next instant a muscular arm encircled her waist, and she was lifted bodily from under her blanket, lifted as easily as she might lift a blade of grass.

Sluggish from sleep and her injury, Lou was slow to react. Belatedly, she began to struggle, but by then the abyss of the night had closed around them and she was being borne at bewildering speed up the mountain.

The creature had her!

The thought struck Lou numb. She stopped struggling and twisted to try and glance back at the clearing and see if Zach was still alive. She could not conceive of him letting the creature take her. The only conclusion, then, was that the thing had killed him.

A pervasive sadness overcame her. She felt sick to her stomach but was able to swallow the bitter bile back down. Tears started to well, but she blinked them away and concentrated on her plight. Her fear was fading. Now she had purpose. Now she would bide her time and when her chance came, she would slay the thing that had killed the man she loved.

Lou loved Zach dearly, loved him more than she had ever deemed it possible to love anyone; more, even, than she had loved her father and mother, and her love for them had been boundless. Or maybe it was better to say it was a *different* kind of love rather than the *degree*.

That was it, Lou decided. Love for a husband was not the same as love for a parent. Both were deep and abiding in their way.

The realization of what she was doing almost made Lou laugh. Here she was, being abducted by God-knew-what, and instead of fighting and screaming, she was thinking about the nature of love. But she soon discovered there was little she could do even if she wanted to. The arm that encircled her also clamped her own arms to her side so that she could only move her wrists and hands, and then barely enough to touch whatever had her. She could not hurt it in any way. When she did touch it, she shivered, for her fingers encountered matted hair much like the hair of an animal. But whatever had taken her was human. It had to be. Animals did not have arms and legs.

That the cries they had heard were produced by human vocal cords added to her fear. What manner of human could it be? Or was she jumping to conclusions? Lou asked herself. Was the creature *inhuman*? Lou never lent much credence to tales of spooks and hobgoblins. Oh, she heard the stories, growing up, but she regarded them in the same vein as she did tales of pixies and fairies and magic carpets.

A sudden violent jar ended Lou's reverie. Her abductor had tripped and nearly fallen. Inadvertently, its grip around her middle tightened like a vise. Her insides were fit to burst. Then the creature righted itself and the vise eased.

Lou craned her neck and saw the light of their campfire, much smaller than before. Her abductor had covered a lot of ground. The sight galvanized her into thrashing her legs and pumping her forearms, but she had no more effect than a kitten would in the grip of a mountain lion. Her captor continued climbing at the same breakneck pace.

The smell was awful. The creature gave off the foulest odor this side of a skunk. It was so rank that several times when Lou breathed too deep, she came close to gagging. Its matted hair, so bristly and coarse, suggested it was unacquainted with the concept of bathing.

Lou tried to tell if her pistols were tucked under her belt. They had been there when she fell asleep. She definitely had her knife, unless the thing had disarmed her before it grabbed her. The knife fit snugly and never fell out.

Lou stared at the receding flames below. Maybe Zach was still alive. Maybe he was hurt, lying wounded, bleeding his life out with every second she was carried farther and farther away. She hoped not. She would rather he were dead than have him suffer.

A question jumped out of the borders of her mind, a question she had refused to ask herself because one of the possible answers was too horrible to contemplate: What did the creature intend to do with her? That it had not killed her outright suggested another purpose. Would it kill her later? Would it eat her? Or was there a more sinister design?

Lou was no babe in the woods. She knew what men sometimes did in the heat of pillage and violence. The very word was odious. It was perhaps the one thing women dreaded most. A violation of the body and the mind so deep, so personal, most women never fully recovered. Her father once told her that men sometimes felt the same, that if a man was beaten or had something he valued stolen, a man felt the same despair and ache deep in his being that a woman felt when a man forced himself on her, but Lou doubted that. Violation was hideous in the extreme. It was the hurt of hurts, a ravaging of all that a woman was.

Her captor abruptly stopped.

Lou tensed and tried to see its face, but her back was to it and she could not twist far enough. She gathered it was staring down the mountain, maybe listening to hear if they were pursued. In which case Zach must still be alive. Or maybe it was only catching its breath.

The creature moved on, but now at a slightly slower pace.

The cold air made Lou yearn for her blankets. To take her mind off the chill and the smell and the pain, she thought about what she would do when the thing finally released her. Inwardly, she smiled. She was a woman, and some claimed women were frail, but she was living proof that was not the case. She would kill the thing that had her, or die trying.

The air grew colder. To the east a pale tinge marked the advent of dawn. She tried to turn her head to see, but the hand over her mouth squeezed so hard she thought her jaw would break.

Time crawled by on snails of worry.

Dawn was not far off when her captor veered toward a thicket. Lou barely had time to turn her face so her eyes would not be poked out before they plunged in. The next thing she knew, she was flat on her back with the thing on top of her. Panicked, she tried to beat at it with her fists, but she could not move her arms. She could not move anything. When it did not seek to molest her, she subsided. Soon its rhythmic breathing told her it was asleep.

Lou was flabbergasted. She pushed against it,

but she was hopelessly pinned. The stink, the pressure, were nearly unbearable. They only got worse as the sun climbed the sky. Again and again she sought to slip out from under the beast. She actually got a leg free, only to have her abductor stir and growl and cuff her so hard she nearly blacked out.

Without exception, it was the longest day of Lou's life. She sweated as she had never sweated. Her ribs ached to the point of collapse.

Twilight was falling when the thing abruptly rose with her in its arm. Once again she was subjected to the ordeal of being toted like a sack of flour.

Hours elapsed. Midnight came and went and still the thing loped on, as tireless as a steam engine.

Without any warning, Lou was roughly dumped on the ground. She landed on her right elbow, and her entire arm flared with torment. When she looked up, her captor was a black mass against a backdrop of white.

The glacier reared above them, an ice cliff higher than the tallest tree. It appeared to be as smooth as glass, but that proved deceptive, as the creature demonstrated by once again scooping her up and doing the impossible; it began to climb the ice.

Her cheek scraped the cold cliff face. To keep from having her face rubbed raw, Lou pressed her head against the thick hair that covered the creature's chest.

They did not climb to the top. They only climbed halfway, to what Lou took to be a ledge, until the thing let go of her and she sat up. The gaping maw of a cave confronted her, a cave of ice formed out of the glacier's cold heart. The creature's lair, Lou deduced, and shivered anew, but not from the cold.

The thing growled and loomed over her.

Instinctively, Lou shrank back, but she had nowhere to go. She was inches from the edge. If she weren't careful she would plummet over the side, and no one could survive a fall from that height.

An arm reached for her. Lou resisted an impulse to swat it aside. She must let the creature think she had given up. Fingers plucked at her hair. The creature bent down and sniffed. Its breath was putrid, worse than its body odor, which hardly seemed possible. It sniffed her hair, her neck, her shoulders.

Lou wished she could see it clearly. Or *him*, for now there could be no mistake whatsoever. It was a man. A huge man, with great stooped shoulders as wide as a bull's. She thought maybe something was wrong with its legs since it always moved with an odd shuffling gait, but up close its legs appeared to be all right. Thick as tree trunks, they were, with no bent ankles or other signs of crippling.

Suddenly the thing grabbed Lou by the hair and turned to drag her. The only thing was, she always wore her hair cropped short, so short that her captor could not get a good grip. He had only dragged her a few steps when he lost his hold.

"Damn you!" Lou snapped, her scalp a welter of pain. She rubbed her head and sat up. "You had no call to do that."

The creature/thing/man did not move or make a sound. It stared, its eyes glittering pits, breathing heavily as if its exertions had caught up with it.

"What do you want?" Lou demanded. "Do you speak English?" When it just stood there, she tried Shoshone. Zach had been teaching her, and while she was nowhere near as adept as his mother at learning other languages, she could get by. She also knew a smattering of Spanish but that, too, failed to provoke a reply. "Can you even talk?"

The sky to the east was brightening. The thing glanced up and growled, as if the break of day disturbed it. Grabbing Lou's arm, it pulled her to the mouth of the cave.

Lou dug in her heels. "No! I don't want to!" But she might as well have railed against a boulder or a tree. The thing ignored her and hauled her after it.

"Oh God," Lou breathed. The moment would soon be upon her. She groped at her belt and was filled with dismay to find both pistols were gone. But not her knife. She gripped the hilt but did not draw it. She would wait until her abductor sought to fondle her. Then she would bury the blade and pray for the best.

Lou could not see her hand in front of her face. She had the impression they were in a tunnel. The ice floor sloped down and turned to the right. The walls widened, the roof was lost in ink. She was peering up trying to get some idea of how big the cavern was when the thing unexpectedly growled and tossed her aside.

Lou collided with an ice wall. It hurt, but not that much. Sitting up, she took stock. She still had her knife, thank God. She heard the thing moving about, but she could not see it. The sounds ceased. Total silence descended. She could not hear the wind, she could not hear anything.

If she had to guess, Lou would say the thing had lain down to rest. But where? She moved her legs back and forth, but nothing was there. "Where are you?" she asked, thinking it might grunt or otherwise give itself away. The silence mocked her.

One thing was for sure. Lou was not going to sit there and wait for it to get its hands on her again. The tunnel was to her left. If she could reach it, if she could only reach it, she might escape.

Lou strained her ears as she had never strained them before. For a while there was nothing, absolutely nothing. Then came soft but heavy breathing, regular and slow. He/It was asleep.

The next instant the ice cave brightened perceptibly. Not much, not more than a shade, but enough to tell her the sun had risen and light was filtering into the tunnel, which faced east.

An insight struck her, the reason they only heard the howls and roars at night. The thing slept during the day. If she could get past it, she could be long gone before it woke up, provided she could somehow descend the ice cliff.

One problem at a time, Lou cautioned herself. She rose, probing above her in case the roof was lower than she thought it was. She did not bump her head. Turning to the left, she ventured a tentative step. Nothing happened. The creature did not let out a sound other than the regular breathing.

I can do it, Lou told herself, and took another step. She was careful not to scrape her soles on the ice. She did not know, but the thing might have the same keen senses as a bear or a mountain lion.

Each step played havoc with Lou's nerves. She hardly breathed, she was so scared. Her right hand was glued to the hilt of her knife. She would take a step, pause to listen, then take another. Step. Listen. Step. Listen. She must have gone ten feet and still she could not make out the tunnel. But it was there. It was there!

The breathing grew louder.

Three more steps, and Lou suddenly stopped. The breathing seemed to be coming from almost at her feet. She noticed a vague outline, and beyond it, the suggestion of an arch. Elation coursed through her. It had to be the tunnel!

Unthinking, Lou took another step and nearly cried out when her toe bumped something. Something that stirred and made a noise as of heavy lips smacking together.

The thing *was* at her feet.

Lou divined what the creaute had done. It had stretched out across the opening. To reach the tunnel she had to step over it.

A chill gripped her, a chill that had nothing to do with her surroundings. The ice cave was surprisingly warm. No, the chill was spawned by the price she would pay if she blundered. She bent down, trying to make out exactly where the thing lay, but all she could distinguish in the gloom was its giant bulk. Lord, but he/it was huge! She always thought her father-in-law was big, but the thing at her feet dwarfed him.

Lou inched to the right, thinking there might be a gap she could slip through. But no. She came to the ice wall. The creature's legs blocked her from getting by. Undeterred, she crept to the left. Again she came to where the cave and the tunnel merged, and again she was blocked, this time by his/its shoulders and outstretched arms.

She moved back to about where its waist should be. She raised a leg but lowered it again. The thing was too immense for her to step over. She might be able to jump over it. But if she misjudged, or it heard her, there was no telling what it would do to her.

Lou was standing there debating what to do when the problem was taken out of her hands.

With a grunt, the creature rolled over and sat up.

Chapter Twelve

When Zach's horse flagged, he switched to Lou's. He pushed them harder than he ever pushed any horse, pushed them almost cruelly, but the entire day went by and not once did he catch sight of Lou and whatever had taken her. He wanted to press on after the sun went down, but he had to face the truth; both mounts were about done in. If he kept going, he risked riding them into the ground.

Zach could not have that. He needed them, needed to reach the glacier as swiftly as humanly possible. Accordingly, chafing at the necessity, along about midnight he drew rein on the bank of the stream, stripped both exhausted horses, and settled down to catch what sleep he could, which proved to be precious little. He could not stop thinking about Lou, about what she might be going through. About whether she was alive or dead.

Fear ate at Zach like termites at wood. He tossed. He turned. Every now and again he got up and paced, then lay back down. Finally he dozed off, but his rest was brief. He was up again an hour before dawn, saddling the horses. He did not bother with breakfast. He had no appetite.

The horses were sluggish. They had not recovered and were loath to suffer a repeat of the day before. But Zach was relentless. He had squandered precious hours. He would not waste more.

Zach focused on the glacier. He squinted against the glare, squinted for so long and so hard, his eyes hurt. He spied a few elk. He spotted deer. But he did not see Lou or the thing that took her.

Images filled Zach's mind. Blood-drenched images of what he would do to her abductor when he caught up with them. It was going to die. As surely as the sun rose and set each day, as surely as the mountains existed, it was going to die in agony, and take a long time in the dying.

Zach had never wanted to kill anyone or anything as much as he hankered to slay her captor. When he and Louisa first met, she used to tease that he was too bloodthirsty for his own good. If she only knew. He had suppressed a lot of urges since they'd wed, urges to eliminate those who posed a threat. But he would not suppress the urge this time. He would let the violence out, with a vengeance.

The day waxed slower than melting candles. Both horses became lathered with sweat. Zach's buckskins clung wetly to his body. He yearned to stop and rest, but fear drove him on, fear that he would be too late, that he would fail Lou when she needed him most.

At times like this, Zach almost regretted living in the wilderness. Danger was always a misstep away. Unforeseen perils were all too common. Lou would be safer east of the Mississippi, where the large meat-eaters had been practically eliminated. That, and nearly all the hostiles tribes had been pushed west or wiped out.

But as much as Zach loved Lou, and he loved her with all his heart and mind and strength, he loved the wilderness almost as much. He had spent his whole life in the wilds. To him, encountering a bear or a mountain lion was no more unusual than putting on his moccasins. They just *were*, and had to be dealt with as the occasion arose.

The same with unfriendly Indians. Part Shoshone himself, Zach not only understood the warrior culture of many of the tribes, he reveled in it. To him, there were few experiences more exhilarating than counting coup. Although of late it had admittedly lost some of its appeal.

Again, though, it was part and parcel of not only his life but life in general on the frontier. Everyone who ferried the Mississippi River knew they took their life in their hands the moment they set foot on the western shore. It was as inescapable as breathing. Complaining about it, wishing conditions were different, was useless. Like the wild beasts that roamed the plains and forests, the tribes who lived there had to be accepted for what they were. Some, like the Flatheads and the Shoshones, were friendly. Some, like the Sioux and the Blackfeet, were not.

It was a lesson Zach learned at an early age. In that regard he was more like his mother's people than his father's. Whites were never satisfied. They were always trying to impose their will on their surroundings rather than accept and adapt to those surroundings. There were exceptions, of course, his father and Shakespeare being two of the more notable.

Still, acceptance did not bring peace of mind. Especially not at moments like this, when his wife's life hung in the balance.

The glacier was a lot nearer. It was not a solid mass of ice as Zach had thought, but was mantled with snow near the summit. Serpentine in shape, it wound between high canyon walls that served to shade it for most of the day from the heat of the sun, and probably accounted for why it had not melted in the eons since it was formed. An ice precipice formed the lower end. If the thing was up there somewhere, it could see for miles.

At the thought, Zach reined toward some aspens. He had to get under cover before it was too late, if it wasn't already. He cursed himself for a fool. The lack of sleep, and worry, had conspired to make him careless. He could only hope the creature had not spotted him.

Dismounting, Zach threaded through the aspens to a belt of scrub brush and boulders. Darting from cover to cover, he worked his way to within a few hundred feet of the ice cliff.

Now what? Zach asked himself. The glacier was half a mile long and about half that wide. To search every square foot would take weeks. There must be cracks, crevices, even caves the thing could hide in. How was he to find it in all that icy expanse?

He was mulling over his options when the canyon walls that overlooked the glacier echoed to a piercing scream.

Lou was not a fainter. She had never fainted in her life. But she came uncomfortably close when the man-thing grunted and sat up. All the blood seemed to rush from her head and her senses swam in a haze of fright. Her knees started to buckle but she firmed them, and froze.

The monster's back was to her. It was staring into the tunnel, not into the cave. All it had to do was turn and it would see her, but to her astonishment and relief, it lay back down, placed its head on an arm, and within moments was breathing loudly and rhythmically once again.

Lou began to tremble, her whole body, from her head to her feet. She willed herself to stop but she couldn't. A reaction, she figured, to nearly being caught. After a while the quaking ceased, but she felt weak and short of breath, as if she had run a couple of miles. Why that should be, she could not say.

The important thing was that she could still escape. All she had to do was get past *it*. But how, when it blocked the tunnel? She leaned forward, careful not to breathe too loudly, and noticed that when the creature had lain back down, only one of its arms blocked the left wall. The other arm was curled under its head.

Lou edged closer. Gingerly, she lifted her right foot and placed it on the other side of the arm.

The creature didn't stir. She raised her other foot and was almost over when the man-brute snorted and rolled onto its back.

Lou saw its eyes glare up at her. She braced for a blow or the rending of claws. But all it did was glare. Her nerves about to break, she balled her fists to defend herself as best she could. Still the thing lay there. Unable to stand the strain any longer, she went to leap over it. That was when she saw its eyes were closed. It was still asleep. Her mind had played tricks on her.

Swallowing, Lou silently slunk into the tunnel, placing each foot with care. The farther she went, the lighter the tunnel became. She rounded a bend and nearly burst into tears at the sight of the entrance, ablaze in glorious sunlight. Forgetting herself, she ran.

She had been breathing foul air for so long that the fresh air was flowery sweet. She stood near the edge and spread her arms and breathed deep. But she dared not dawdle. The thing could wake up at any moment.

Lou dropped onto all fours and peered over the edge. The height was dizzying. How the creature had managed to climb the ice face baffled her. Then she saw them; niches chopped out of the ice, niches that could be used as handholds and footholds. Flattening, she reached down and ran her hand over the top niche. It was deep enough for a good grip, yet even so, it was ice, and all it would take was a single slip and she would fall to her death.

Lou sat up and glanced at the tunnel. What

choice did she have? It was either try to climb down or wait for the thing to have its way with her.

Steeling herself, Lou slowly eased her legs over. She carefully probed with her right toe until she found the top niche. They were spaced uncomfortably far apart. She had to stretch her left leg to reach the next one. Then came the worst part, the part that required all the courage she possessed. With a silent prayer, she slid over the side and clung to her perch.

She felt the fear take hold, felt her limbs start to weaken. *No!* she screamed at herself. She would not give in. She would be strong. She would do what needed to be done. Giving in was for the timid, and she had never been a quitter. If she had learned anything from her father, it was that a person never, ever gave up. So long as she had breath in her body she would do what she had to in order to survive.

Lou glanced down. Her newfound resolve nearly dissolved at the sight of the ground so very far below. Turning her face to the ice, she began her descent. First one foot, then the other, then an arm, then the other. It was wisest to move slowly to reduce the risk of slipping, but she did not have the luxury. She must reach the bottom quickly.

She moved her leg, her other leg, her arm, her other arm. Already her shoulders were aching. She lowered her leg, then heard a faint sound from above. Looking up, she did something she had rarely ever done; she screamed.

The creature was staring down at her. Its huge head was enfolded in a bearskin and only part of the face was visible; its glittering eyes, a long, wide nose, a mouth rimmed with teeth in which bits of flesh were stuck. It was squinting at her, and as she met its fearful gaze, its eyes started to water.

Lou did not understand at first. Not until it glanced up at the sky and recoiled as if it had been struck. Then it hit her. The thing could not take the sun. It had lived in the dark of the ice cave and prowled in the dark of night for so long, its eyes were extremely sensitive to bright light. Smiling, she said fiercely, "Come get me, you devil, and I hope you fall!"

She got her wish. A leg like a tree trunk slid over the edge and a foot covered by a bear-paw moccasin dug into a niche. It was coming after her. Only then did she realize that if the thing did fall, it would fall on her.

Lou glanced down. She could not possibly reach the bottom before the abomination reached her. She tried anyway. Left with no recourse, she descended faster, too fast to be safe. Ten feet. Twenty feet. And still so many more to go. Again she glanced up.

The thing was after her, yes, but it was descending much more slowly. Its eyes were almost shut and it was feeling for the niches one by one. At that rate it would take forever to reach the ground.

Encouraged, Lou continued. In the light, the thing was not quite as fearsome. It was a man, as she had surmised, a huge man dressed in a bearskin with the claws still attached. She could see a mark on the edge of the pelt that she guessed was from Zach's shot, but if the creature had been wounded, he showed no sign of it. But that mystery along with who he was and why he lived in the glacier would have to wait.

She was lowering her leg when she thought she heard a shout. Dismissing it as another trick of her mind or a trick of the wind, she lowered her other leg. Then faint but clear came a yell.

"Lou! Lou! I'm coming!"

Louisa looked down. Zach was racing toward the ice cliff and waving his arms. Now she was the one with tears in her eyes, tears of love and joy. Blinking them back, she kept descending.

Zach's next shout held a note of alarm. "Lou! Look out! Above you!"

Lou raised her face to look up just as flecks of ice rained down. The man-thing was not moving slowly anymore. It was descending with incredible swiftness. A cry escaped her. It would be on her in moments.

That was when a rifle boomed and a heavy slug cored the ice inches from the creature's head. It stopped and glanced at Zach. The bearskin hood fell away, revealing its face and head fully for the first time.

Lou gasped. The features were human but the head was strangely misshapen. The crown was sunken, as if the skull had caved in, and the sides bulged. A shock of filthy black hair grew at all different angles. The eyes were still watering but not as much, and in those eyes was the gleam of something Lou could not quite describe. Madness? Seething hate? They were more like animal eyes than human eyes. She saw no trace of the deeper intelligence that marked a human being, only the savagery such as she might see in the eyes of a grizzly or a wolverine.

The moment passed. With amazing speed, the creature snarled and went up the cliff onto the ledge. It was out of sight before Zach could reload.

Which was fine by Lou. She resumed her descent. Twice her feet slipped, but each time she had a firm grip with her hands and was able to cling on and jam her foot into a niche.

Zach was waiting at the bottom. He had the Hawken to his shoulder, ready in case the man-beast came after her. He smiled each time she looked down, and each smile brought warmth to her heart.

It seemed like hours but it could not have been more than ten minutes when Lou heard him say, "You're almost there, hon. Just a little bit more."

Another few moments and his arms were around her and Lou turned and her cheek was on his chest and he was stroking her hair.

"You did it. You're safe now."

Lou knew better. As soon as the sun went down, if not sooner, the monster would be after them. Unless they put a lot of miles between them and the glacier, they would have to go through the whole thing all over again: being chased, being hunted, and maybe, God help her, being caught. She pulled back. "We have to get out of here."

Nodding, his arm around her shoulders, Zach led her toward a stand of aspens. "Are you all right?" he worriedly asked. "I mean, that thing didn't—" He did not finish his question.

"No, it didn't," Lou said.

"It's a man, isn't it? I didn't get a good look."

"A man," Lou confirmed. "But whether he is human, I can't rightly say." Suddenly she was tired. So tired her eyelids grew heavy with the sleep she had been denied. Yawning, she shook herself. She would sleep when they were in the clear, not before.

Zach was saying how he had ridden like the wind to reach the glacier, and how he had about despaired of finding her when he heard her scream. They entered the aspens and he stopped and looked around in confusion.

"What's the matter?" Lou asked.

"The horses," Zach said.

"What about them?"

"They're gone."

Chapter Thirteen

Zach tried to remember if he had tied the horses and couldn't recall. He had been so worried about Lou, he had not been thinking about anything else. Now he ran another dozen yards to a spot that afforded a view of the slope below, hoping to spot the horses, but they were nowhere to be seen. They were probably well on their way to the valley floor, to the cabin and their corral. "Damn."

Lou was at his side. "No use crying over spilt milk," she said, with an anxious glance at the glacier. "We have to get as far away as we can before the sun goes down. He will be after us."

"He?"

Lou related her ordeal as they jogged down the mountain. Fatigue had taken its toll, so she could not go as fast as she normally would. In an all too short span she had to go even slower. Her legs had become wooden and her feet ached abominably. She pushed on, though, until her blood was pounding in her ears and she was on the verge of collapse. Stopping at last, she bent over with her hands on her knees. "I'm sorry. I can't take another step. You should go on without me."

Zach looked at her. "That has to be the silliest thing you have ever said to me."

"You can go a lot farther without me," Lou said.

"Do you seriously expect me to leave you?" Zach snorted. "You are my wife. I'll stay by your side, come what may."

"You don't understand. This thing, this person, he's not like anyone or anything we have ever gone up against."

"So? If he is flesh and blood, he can bleed, and if he can bleed, we can kill him," Zach said, wagging his Hawken for emphasis.

"But all I have is my knife," Lou said.

"Thanks for reminding me." One by one Zach drew his pistols and handed them to her.

"I can't take both."

"You can and you will," Zach insisted. "They're .55 caliber. Up close they can stop a griz. They'll stop this thing, too."

Lou tucked the big flintlocks under her belt. "We still have a few hours of daylight left. We should keep going."

Zach gazed at the spruce trees and the brush. "You rest awhile. You're wore out."

"We can't afford to." Lou sucked in a breath and prepared to move on, but he clasped her arm.

"I mean it. Rest." Zach examined the ground, then moved off, saying, "I'll be right back."

Lou did not like being left alone. She nervously

scoured their back trail. The thing hated the sun, but it might come after them anyway. The mere thought of being in its clutches again terrified her. She nearly gave a start when Zach unexpectedly emerged holding a short length of tree branch about as thick as his forearm. "What is that for?"

"A little surprise for your admirer." Zach drew his bowie and chopped at one end of the branch, whittling it to a sharp point. Then, kneeling, he dug a hole slightly larger than the feet of their adversary's and about eighteen inches deep. He resharpened the tip, then embedded the stick, point up, and covered the hole with brush and a few thin pine limbs.

"Even if that works," Lou commented, "it won't do more than slow him down."

"Which is exactly what we want." Zach rose and stepped back to appraise his handiwork. "Walk around the hole a few times so your scent is good and strong."

Lou did so, then urged, "We really should keep going. I can manage now." She started off through the woods.

Zach let her think she had him fooled. He could tell she was worn out and he watched her closely without being obvious. She was tough, his wife, and they covered more than a mile before he saw her legs wobble and heard her breath catch in her throat. "Let's rest again," he said, and stopped without waiting for her to agree.

Leaning against a tree, Lou closed her eyes. "I'm sorry," she gasped. "I'm plumb tuckered out."

"This is as far as we go, then."

"We can't stop," Louisa puffed. "You have no idea what we are up against."

"Give me more credit," Zach said. He had fought grizzlies. He had fought a wolverine. He had gone up against the Blackfeet and the Sioux. He had tangled with renegade whites. "I won't let the son of a bitch harm you," he vowed.

Lou wearily smiled. He meant well, but he had not seen the thing close up. He did not appreciate how huge it was, how tireless and strong.

Zach tilted his head back and regarded the spruce she was leaning against. "Take a nap. I'll wake you at sunset."

"I couldn't sleep if I tried," Lou said. She was too overwrought. But she did sit with her back to the bole and mop at her face with a sleeve. "I must look a sight."

"You're as pretty as the day we met," Zach said, and meant it. In some indefinable fashion, he found her more lovely as time went on. It mystified him. He had figured that when two people lived together and saw one another day in and day out, they would get so used to each other that their allure would lose some of its appeal. But that was not the case. Lou truly was more lovely to him now than she had ever been. He never tired of admiring her when she was not aware. At night he would lie and gaze at her for hours, feasting on her beauty, and the marvel that she had taken him, out of all the men in the world, for her husband. He adored her, and he was not ashamed to admit it—to himself.

Lou mustered a grin. "You are the most wonderful liar. But I thank you anyway." She turned serious. "I hope you have a plan. We can't just sit here and wait for it."

"That is exactly what we are going to do," Zach responded. "Now close your eyes and try to sleep."

"I can't, I tell you," Lou said. To humor him she closed them anyway and took a few deep breaths to relax. The next she knew, a hand was on her shoulder, gently shaking her, and she opened her eyes to find the woodland shrouded in the gray of falling twilight.

Zach smiled down at her. "For someone who couldn't sleep, you snored loud enough to wake the dead."

Lou pushed to her feet. "No, no, no. You shouldn't have let me." She gazed up the mountain, but she could not see the glacier for the trees. "It will be after us soon if it isn't already."

"Let it come." Zach patted the trunk she had been leaning against. "I'll give you a boost. Climb until I say to stop. I'll be right behind you."

Lou craned her neck. The tree was thirty feet high, maybe more. "What good will it do? Surely you don't intend to spend the night up there?"

"Surely I do," Zach said. "There is only one way for your friend to get at us, and we have three guns and plenty of ammunition."

"I don't know," Lou said dubiously. But it might work. The thing was a lot heavier than they were. No matter how quietly it tried to climb, they would hear it, or feel the tree shake.

"If you can think of a better place to make a stand, I'm listening," Zach said. He particularly liked that he would be below her. To reach Lou, the bastard had to get past him.

"I can't," Lou admitted. The only idea she could think of was to find a large boulder and stand with their backs to it, but there was no guarantee they would get off a shot when the thing rushed them out of the dark.

Zach grinned. "Then up you go, wench." He leaned his Hawken against the tree and cupped his hands.

Lou was raising her leg when they both heard it. From high up the mountain rose the ululating cry of the creature. It had left its lair and was after them. She could not suppress a gasp.

"I won't let it hurt you," Zach said again.

Lou smiled but she did not share his confidence. She hooked her foot in his hands and reached up. Another moment and she was perched on a low limb. He swung up beside her and they sat there, their shoulders touching.

"I'm sorry this happened."

"It's hardly your fault," Lou said, puzzled. "I was the one who wanted to see the glacier up close." She shuddered. "Well, I got my wish."

"Not that," Zach said. "I'm sorry this has spoiled your plans. Starting our family will have to wait."

"Only until we get home," Lou teased. "Then I'm holding you to your promise if I have to rip your clothes off."

"My wife, the hussy," Zach joked.

Lou giggled, then realized what he was doing, and letting go of the limb, she hugged him. "Thank you. I needed that."

"Just so you know, I won't go back on my word. A promise is a promise. With a little luck and a lot of hard work on my part, in a month or two you will be in the family way."

"Hard work, huh?" Lou repeated, and chortled. "Since when is *that* work? You men love it and you know it."

"We don't complain," Zach said.

Another howl that was not a howl caused Lou to stiffen and gaze into the darkening murk. "I think that is what he had in mind. He took me to be his mate."

"You're spoken for," Zach said. He did not mention how relieved he was that she had not been molested. It had been his innermost fear.

"That works both ways," Lou said, and kissed him on the cheek. "When my father died I was crushed. I was all alone in the world. I didn't know what I would do, where I would go. Then you came along. You came out of nowhere and won my heart, and I have not regretted a day since."

Neither had Zach, which was peculiar, since he had long thought he would live his life a bachelor. He had more than a few failings, not the least of which was his temper, and when he was younger he could not conceive of a woman, any woman, willing to put up with him.

Lou cleared her throat and reached for a higher limb. "We should get ready for when he shows."

"It will be a while yet." Hours, Zach reckoned.

Already climbing, Lou said over her shoulder, "It can't be long enough to suit me."

Nate King liked to think he was as good a judge of human nature as the next coon. He made a habit of studying other people as he studied his books, and reading between the lines where it was called for. He was trying to read between the lines now.

Something was bothering Neota. Nate knew the warrior fairly well, and liked him. The Ute had saved his life once, a debt Nate would not forget. The first day on their climb to the glacier, he tried several times, using sign, to engage the warrior in conversation. But Neota was uncharacteristically moody, and refused to be drawn into lengthy sign talk. He responded with the sign equivalents of yes and no to most of Nate's overtures.

That night they camped in the shelter of a hummock that spared them the worst of the wind. Nate shared his pemmican and slices of bread from a loaf Winona had packed. They chewed in somber silence, Neota lost inside himself, until Nate cleared his throat to get the other's attention, and signed, "Question. You all right?"

"I good," Neota signed.

Nate decided enough was enough. "You sign talk two tongues," he bluntly signed, in effect saying that Neota was lying.

Neota glanced up sharply and darkened with anger, but the color slowly drained and he bowed his head and sighed.

Patiently waiting for the Ute to look up, Nate signed, "We be friends. Friends talk straight tongue."

A full five minutes went by before Neota's fingers flowed in sign. As was his custom, Nate mentally filled in missing words, the better to communicate. In essence, Neota said, "I wish you and your family had not moved to this valley."

"It is a fine valley with plenty of water and game."

"It is bad medicine. The Utes think so. The Crows think so. The Nez Perce think so. But whites never listen to the red man."

"My wife likes it here and she is Shoshone. Blue Water Woman likes it here and she is a Flathead."

"The Flatheads live far away, in the country of the white fish lake. They have never visited this valley. They do not know."

"The Shoshones live closer."

"But they, too, did not know this valley was here. If they did, they would say it was bad medicine, the same as the Utes and the Crows and the Nez Perce."

"Perhaps they would," Nate conceded. "But why are you sad my family came? Because of To-Ma?"

"We thought him long dead," Neota signed.

"Maybe it is not him we hear at night. Maybe it is something else."

"It is him."

"Are you sad because he did not die?" Nate asked, seeking to make sense of the contradiction. "I should think you would be happy. He is one of your own, whether his brain is in a whirl or not." "Brain in a whirl" was the sign equivalent for "crazy."

"I am sad because I must hunt him."

"Then I should go on alone," Nate proposed. "You go back to your people and leave it to me."

"I cannot."

"Give me one good reason. You have already done more for him than most would have done."

A bitter laugh rasped from Neota's lips. "Yes, I did a lot for him. I killed To-Ma once. Now, because your family has moved to this valley, I must kill him again."

Chapter Fourteen

The predators were abroad. The night was their element. In the dark they hunted unseen, pounced with lightning speed, and slew with ravenous abandon. From Canada to Mexico, from dusk until dawn was when the darkling legion filled their bellies.

They did not go unheard. The night was a mad chorus of roars, shrieks, and snarls, mixed with the bleat of hapless prey.

Zach King was so used to it that, normally, he did not give the noturnal marauders much thought. They simply *were*, like the mountains and the air he breathed, and must be taken as a matter of course. But on this particular night the bedlam ate at his nerves.

Somewhere out there was a predator like no other. Somewhere close, and coming closer. They had not heard its eerie cry for a while, but that could be because the thing did not want to give itself away.

The tree rustled to a gust of chill wind. Zach had his back to the trunk and both legs wrapped around a limb and he was in no danger of slipping. Raising his head, he asked, "How are you doing up there?"

Lou had one arm wrapped around the trunk and the other over a limb above her. "I'm covered with goose bumps. It's freezing."

"It's not that cold," Zach said, although now and again he shivered. "Try not to think about it, and you'll feel warmer."

"And if I try not to think of that awful creature, maybe I won't worry as much," Lou said insincerely.

"We haven't heard it in a while."

"It's out there. It's probably listening to us right this moment. Listening, and biding its time."

Zach patted his Hawken. "Let it bide all the time it wants. I'm ready."

"Funny how we talk about him as if he's a wild beast of some kind," Lou remarked.

"That's how he acts. Didn't you say he didn't speak a word to you the whole time you were with him?"

"I don't think he can speak," Lou said. "All he does is howl and roar and grunt."

"Then he is a beast, or the next thing to it."

A wolf raised a lonesome lament to the west and was answered by a kindred lupine spirit to the south.

"I wish we were home in bed," Lou said wistfully. "I wish we were warm and snuggly and without a care in the world."

"In a week we'll be home," Zach mentioned. Even on foot it shouldn't take longer than that.

"It might as well be a year."

Zach had seldom heard his wife sound so dejected. A yearning came over him to take her into his arms, but all he could do was squeeze her leg. "It's not like you to give up. We aren't dead yet."

"And I don't want us to be," Lou said softly. "I would give anything—"

A hideous wail shattered the night, a wail of pain and rage in nearly equal measure. It rose to a shrill apex and then fell to a guttural growl that was snuffed out as abruptly as a candle. The silence that fell in its wake was all the more unsettling because it was total and complete.

"Your stake!" Lou exclaimed.

"Let's hope."

"Then it's not here yet," Lou said, overjoyed. "Maybe now it won't come at all. Not if it's hurt and bleeding."

"Maybe," Zach said. They should be so lucky. The thing, man, whatever it was, had shown remarkable persistence. It wanted Louisa, and he doubted it would relent this side of the grave.

"We'll give it another two hours," Lou said. "If it isn't here by then, it's not coming."

"We'll give it until dawn," Zach disagreed. "Better safe than sorry, as my father never tires of saying."

Lou happened to look up just as a shooting star blazed across the heavens. "Oh, look!" she cooed.

"My grandmother used to say they are a good omen."

Not the Shoshones, Zach remembered. Personally, he was not one to believe in omens, good or bad. They smacked of superstition. His father had taught him enough about the science of the whites to make him skeptical of various things his mother's people took for granted. That the moon died and came to life again each month, for instance. That eating dog was bad, that eating roasted ants was worse. That worst of all was for a man to stay in a lodge with a woman when it was her time of the month. That weasel skin could ward off evil spirits. That if a woman took pine needles and ground them up and put them in a small pouch around her baby's neck, the baby would always have excellent health. And so on.

"What are you thinking?" Lou asked. "You got awful quiet."

"About omens and such." Zach did not elaborate. He shifted his weight to be more comfortable, then placed the Hawken across his legs, his left hand always on it so it would not slip.

"Have I thanked you for coming after me? I can't recollect."

Zach had to laugh. "Did you think I wouldn't't?"

"In my heart I knew you would," Lou said. "I can always count on you, come what may. Just as you can always count on me. I think folks call that love."

"Shakespeare told me once that love is a man sticking his head in a woman's loop and asking for the privilege of being dragged through a bed of thorns."

"That sounds like something he would say. But you don't hear him complain about being married to Blue Water Woman." Lou sighed. "I hope you and I are as deeply in love as they are when we are their age."

Zach had an ear cocked to the wind. He thought he had heard the crackle of undergrowth in the near-distance.

"The next time I suggest we go up into the high country on a lark, kick me," Lou said.

"The next time you can go by yourself," Zach quipped. The crackling had not been repeated, but the skin between his shoulder blades was prickling as it sometimes did when his intuition flared in warning.

"Do you ever regret taking me for your wife?"

Zach twisted so he could see her face. "Keep up with the silly questions. Amusement is in short supply."

"I'm serious."

"That makes it even sillier," Zach said. "Why do women ask things like that?"

"You men do your share of silly stuff. Remember that night you thought you heard something skulking around our cabin and shot that poor chicken?"

"It should have stayed in the coop where it belonged."

"Or how about that time you were fishing and you left your line in the water and your pole on the shore while you ran inside for a bite to eat, and when you were on your way back out, you saw your pole swim off into the lake?"

"It was pulled in," Zach corrected her. "The fish

had to be as big as a whale. That pole wasn't light."

"Then there was the time—"

"I get the idea." Zach cut her off. "We both do our share of silly stuff. But if we tallied them up, you would win."

"Says the male."

"What is that supposed to mean?" Zach was smiling, but his smile died at the suggestion of sound from close by the spruce. He glanced down but saw only darkness.

"Only that for as long as there have been women and men, women have thought men are peculiar and men have thought women are peculiar."

"And the truth of it is that both are normal," Zach finished for her.

"No. Men *are* peculiar," Lou said, and laughed. But she quickly sobered when the entire tree shook even though the wind had temporarily died. "What was that?" she whispered.

An answer came from below in the form of a rumbling growl much like a grizzly would make, but this was no griz.

"It's found us!" Louisa whispered.

"That it has," Zach said aloud. Whispering was pointless when the brute knew where they were.

"What now?"

"We sit tight and let it make the first move." Waiting went against Zach's grain. He would rather take the fight to the creature. But he had Lou to think of.

The tree shook again, harder. Zach was impressed. He had chosen the spruce because it was big enough and sturdy enough to withstand an avalanche. The strength required to shake it was prodigious.

"Go away!" Lou called down. "Leave us be!"

"That won't do any good," Zach reminded her. "You said yourself it can't talk."

"Not any language that I know," Lou said. "Maybe it knows some other. Why don't you try?"

The shaking had stopped. Certain he was wasting his time, Zach hollered in every tongue he had even a passing acquaintance with: English, Shoshone, Flathead, Nez Perce, Blackfoot, Crow, Dakota, or Sioux as they were called, Apache from the family's time in Santa Fe, and Spanish. He received no reply, not so much as a peep, until he said in Ute, "We come in peace."

A volcano erupted at the base of the tree, a cacophony of snarls and sputters and weird gibbering cries that brought to mind the ravings of a lunatic.

"What did you say?" Lou breathlessly asked when the tirade ceased.

Zach told her. He possessed barely a smattering of Ute, enough to dissuade any Utes he ran into from trying to lift his hair. Or so he hoped. Niwot, the young warrior who had courted his sister for a spell, had taught him. Zach frowned at the memory. He had liked that boy.

The gibberish grew louder, attended by more shaking of the spruce, violent shaking, as if the thing in the bear skin was trying to tear the tree out by the roots.

"Do you think we're safe up here?" Lou dubiously asked.

"He'd have to be as strong as fifty buffalo to

topple us," Zach confidently replied. "Nothing is that strong."

"You hope." Lou's lower lip began quivering and she bit it to stop. Her husband was right, of course. There was no animal anywhere that could knock over a tree that size. Still, she remembered how ungodly powerful it was, and she could not help but tremble.

"If it stays down there, all we have to do is wait it out until dawn," Zach said. "As soon as the sun is up it will hunt cover and we can push on."

"I'll be awful tired by daybreak," Lou noted.

So would Zach but he would do what he had to, up to and including throwing her over his shoulder and carrying her if need be.

The creature fell silent.

"What do you reckon it's doing?" Lou whispered.

"Picking its nose," Zach responded. "How would I know? I have nothing in common with that thing other than an interest in you."

"You're both male."

Despite their plight, Zach chuckled. "You have a high opinion of yourself, wench, if you think everything male wants you."

"Males always want females. It's your nature. And stop calling me wench. You aren't Shakespeare."

"Why can he do it and I can't?"

"All those white hairs of his give him the right." Lou grinned.

A tremor shook the spruce. Not a violent shake like before, but a mild, sustained ripple of movement, *as if something were climbing it.*

"Oh God," Louisa breathed, and put her hands on the pistols.

Zach was staring straight down. He saw nothing at first. Then a bulk acquired nebulous substance at the limit of his vision. He pointed the Hawken but he did not shoot. He wanted it closer, so close he could not possibly miss, so close the force of the slug ripping through its body would blast it from the tree.

"Can you see it?" Lou whispered. Her mouth was dry, her heart hammering. She was trying to be brave, she truly was, but her memories of the lair were too fresh, too vivid.

"Hush," Zach said. The wild man had stopped.

"But can you see him?" Apprehension ate at Lou like acid. Her palms were damp with sweat, her mouth dry.

"Make up your mind," Zach said. "Is this thing an it or a him?"

"I like your word," Lou answered. "It is a Thing. A great, hulking Thing."

"Then that's what we will call it." Zach had the Hawken to his shoulder and his cheek to the stock. If only the Thing would keep climbing.

"What is it doing?"

"Watching us, I think. Maybe making up its mind what it's going to do," Zach said.

"Where is it? I want to see." Lou leaned out to see past her husband and nearly lost her grip. Her heart hammering in her chest, she clutched at a limb just in time.

"Be careful up there," Zach said without looking up. "You fall on me, we fall on the Thing, and we all fall to the ground."

"So long as the Thing is on the bottom when we hit."

Her comment spawned an idea that Zach discarded as loco, but it crept back into his mind, the image searing him with a promise of salvation. But would it really work? he wondered. He imagined letting go and dropping like a boulder on top of the Thing. At the least he would stun it. At the most he might break its neck. He might also break his own. There were a lot of intervening limbs, and the ground was no pillow.

A new tremor agitated the spruce.

Zach's eyes narrowed. He peered down until they ached. There could be no doubt. The bulk had grown larger.

The Thing was on the move.

It was coming for them, and they had nowhere to run, nowhere to hide. Licking his lips, he thumbed back the Hawken's hammer.

Time to do or die.

Chapter Fifteen

Nate thought he understood. Since Neota had led the war party, Neota felt a degree of guilt over To-Ma being struck in the head by that Shoshone warrior during the raid. "You cannot blame yourself. In war a lot happens we cannot control."

"You do not understand. I did not speak with a straight tongue when I told you about To-Ma."

Nate was stunned. For Neota to admit he lied was remarkable; for Neota to lie, unthinkable. Nate had always regarded him as honest as the year was long, and then some.

The story came out in spurts. Neota would talk awhile, then lapse into troubled silence until spurred by a question or two from Nate. Gradually the full truth was revealed.

Neota had not wanted to take To-Ma along. But To-Ma's father was a good friend, and out of that friendship was forged the seed of tragedy. Neota agreed they could go. As a precaution, he took the father aside and advised him to keep a close watch on his oversized son. To-Ma was clumsy and noisy and would not be at all reliable in a situation that called for stealth.

All had gone well, though, until they dismounted to climb the ridge and spy on the Shoshone encampment. To-Ma had talked a lot on the ride there, but then, To-Ma had always been a talker. He could not seem to keep quiet for more than a few shakes of his mount's tail. He chattered about the weather, about the raid, about the Shoshones, about everything and anything. It was annoying. It was more than annoying. Several of the older warriors asked him not to talk so much, Neota among them, but To-Ma babbled on.

One night Neota drew the father from the fire and told him something must be done. The father apologized. To-Ma had always been that way. Ever since the boy learned to talk, there was no shutting him up. The boy could not seem to grasp there were times when talking must not be done.

The father agreed to do what he could, but the next day was a repeat of those that had gone before.

Then they came to the ridge. Neota picked the warriors who would go with him to raid the village. Those he did not pick were to stay behind and guard their mounts. One of those he did not pick was To-Ma.

Neota had the rest of the warriors to think of.

To bring To-Ma would needlessly imperil them.

That should have been the end of it. They snuck close to the Shoshone village and were about to swoop in and help themselves to as many horses as they could drive off when To-Ma appeared and recklessly charged into the herd. He had not obeyed Neota. He had done as he pleased. And because he was big and clumsy and noisy, the Shoshones heard him and a general cry of alarm spread like a prairie wildfire throughout the encampment.

The raid became a fight for their lives. Battling furiously, the Utes retreated in orderly fashion. With one exception. To-Ma refused to give ground. He stood like a boulder among pebbles and would not be budged. And because the other Utes would not desert him, it soon became apparent to Neota that unless something drastic was done, all of them would die.

In the heated swirl of combat, the air filled with dust and shouts and cries of pain, none of the Utes saw Neota dart over to To-Ma. "We must leave!" he shouted at the boy.

Spattered with blood and caked with sweat, a heap of enemies lying at his feet, the giant boy had laughed and said he was staying right there. "We can beat them!" he crowed. "We can beat them all!"

It was preposterous. They were few and the Shoshones were many. As soon as more Shoshone warriors rallied, it would all be over.

Neota was overcome with worry for his raiding party. The Utes were hard pressed. They could not hope to last much longer. Unless something was done, To-Ma's childish stubbornness would cost them dearly. So Neota did the only thing he could think of to do. He looked around to ensure no one was watching. Then, picking up a war club dropped by a slain Shoshone, he glided behind To-Ma and hit the stripling on the back of the head.

Neota never meant to harm the boy. He meant to knock him out. He called for help, shouting that the Shoshones had struck To-Ma down, and the father and others came and lifted the boy and whisked him down the ridge. To-Ma revived enough to ride, and Neota thought all was well. He had saved the war party from being wiped out.

But later the full extent of the boy's head wound became apparent. Pangs of guilt assailed Neota, but he could not bring himself to admit what he had done. The Utes thought the Shoshones were to blame. He let them go on thinking that, while doing all he could to help the father and the boy.

Then came that terrible day when To-Ma committed the most despicable deed an Ute could commit; he killed another Ute. Slew his own father by ripping out his throat with his bare teeth.

There were calls for To-Ma's death. Warriors who had known the boy since he was an infant and watched him grow winter by winter, warriors who had been close friends of the father, urged the boy's destruction. It was for the good of

all the Utes, they argued. To-Ma was too dangerous to be permitted to roam free.

Neota agreed. The boy was a menace. He
should be destroyed. But his was the deciding
vote in council, and when the moment of decision
rested squarely on his shoulders, when all he had
to do was say he agreed and the matter would be
taken out of his hands, he could not say the
words. He could not pronounce death when his
was the hand responsible for the boy's affliction.

Neota stood and gave a speech. Eloquently, he
pleaded for the boy's life, and because of his elo-
quence, and because he was so widely respected,
the Utes conceded to his wish and banished To-
Ma from their kind forever.

Neota's guilt was a crushing weight on his
spirit. In the grip of despair, he moved about the
village in a shadow state, blind to everyone and
everything except his inner torment. The other
Utes thought it noble of him. His grief, they said,
was a measure of his affection for the boy's father.
He was praised for the lie he was living. He was
held in esteem for an act so despicable, he could
not bear to confess the truth.

Neota had his wife to thank for bringing him
out of himself. Her love for him was a tonic that
restored his reason. The harm had been done. He
could not go back and change the past. The future
must be addressed, and to ensure that future, and
ensure To-Ma never again took a Ute life, Neota
proposed bringing the boy to the valley of bad
medicine.

Neota flattered himself he was doing To-Ma a

favor. The boy would not want for water or food. The entire valley was his own private domain. And if there was no one to share it with, well, that was not Neota's fault. He had done all he could. He left the valley with a clear conscience.

Or so Neota told himself.

His conscience was not convinced. From time to time he was plagued by his persistent guilt. He was an honorable man, and he had done that which was not honorable. The shame would bear down on him until he thought he would break under the strain, but he always shook it off and went on with his life as if nothing were amiss. His wife and his children took his occasional moodiness to be the result of the many burdens of leadership. He let them go on thinking that.

Many winters went by. Neota's guilt faded. He shut To-Ma from his mind and got on with his life. Until the day several men who had been off elk hunting came back to reveal that white men and their families were living along the lake in the valley of bad medicine. The very valley to which To-Ma had been banished.

The veil of time was pierced. All the old feelings welled up, as strong, as disturbing, as they ever were. When it was proposed that someone go meet these whites and see what they were like, Neota argued that the whites and their families should be left alone. The Utes had few dealings with whites, ever since a white trapper betrayed their trust and sided with their enemies.

The only white they respected was one named

Grizzly Killer. It was he who helped arrange a truce with the Shoshones. It was he who slew a bear that had become a man-killer.

Neota's surprise was boundless when he learned that the white man who had settled in the valley was none other than Grizzly Killer. Neota could not put it off any longer. He went to the valley, he spent almost a week there, and not once did he come across sign that To-Ma still lived. He thought his inner torment was over at long last.

Then young Niwot was smitten by Evelyn King. Niwot rode to the valley every chance he could to press his suit. It was Niwot, one night in Neota's lodge, who mentioned hearing strange cries from up near the ice, cries unlike any he had ever heard. Niwot, who told Neota that the Kings heard the cries from time to time but had not seen the creature that made them.

A new dread filled Neota. He liked Nate King, liked King's wife and daughter and son. Nate was one of the few whites Neota had met who treated the red man as an equal. Nate was the only white Neota respected as he did his own kind.

It made Neota's worry all the more acute. He realized the source of the cries must be To-Ma. He realized, too, that eventually the Kings and To-Ma would clash. The blood spilled would be on his hands, as was the blood of To-Ma's father, and To-Ma.

There was only one way to end it, Neota decided. He would ride to the valley and confront To-Ma. He must accept the blame for what he had done, and pay the cost, if that is what was demanded of him.

So here they were, their first night out on their climb to the glacier, and Neota could no longer keep the truth to himself. He had to let it free, had to tell someone. What better person than the man whose son and daughter-in-law might fall victim to Neota's folly?

Nate poked at the fire with a stick for the longest while after the Ute warrior was done. Finally he put down the stick so he could use his hands. "Question," he signed. "Why you no speak straight tongue before?"

"My heart much ashamed," Neota signed.

"Many winters To-Ma up there," Nate remarked.

Neota winced as if he had been stabbed. He signed that no one appreciated that fact more than he did. He had wronged the son, he had wronged the father, he had wronged his own people. He had wronged so many that he could not bear the sight of his own reflection. "I bad man," he concluded.

"No. You good man," Nate signed. He went on to say that Neota had only done what he thought was best. Had he not knocked To-Ma out that day long ago, the Shoshones would have over-whelmed the raiding party and every last Ute would have been slain. Neota's quick thinking had saved their lives.

Neota signed that he had hit To-Ma too hard. He thought he had to hit him hard, though. To-Ma was so huge and so powerful that a light blow would not have any effect.

"I mistake," Neota signed. "I kill."

"We all make mistakes," Nate told him. "An act

must be judged by its intent, not the result. Good deeds are not always an accurate measure of the goodness in a person's heart."

Neota was the graven image of torment.

"If blame must be placed," Nate went on, "then the fault lay with the boy's father. To-Ma had not been mature enough to go on the war path. He had a man's body—twice the body of most men—but the mind that ruled the body was the mind of a child. The father should have waited another winter. To-Ma had not been ready for so great a responsibility."

Neota's hands started to move but stopped. He said something in the Ute tongue, his voice choked with emotion, then looked at Nate and slowly signed, "I thank you, Grizzly Killer."

Nate hoped that maybe now the warrior could live with himself. To take the blame for things over which they had no control was pointless. "We will end it," Nate signed.

Neota hunched closer to the fire, his eyes dancing with the reflected light of the crackling flames. "Yes. End it," he signed, his expression as inscrutable as the night.

Sleep proved elusive. Nate tried, but he could not stop thinking of Zach and Lou and what might have happened, or be happening. Dawn was half an hour off when he sat up and puffed on the embers. There was coffee left in the pot, and he could use all he could drink.

Neota yawned, sat up, and stretched. He pointed at the coffeepot and motioned that he would like some, too.

A rosy hue painted the east when they climbed on their horses and jabbed their heels.

Nate took the lead. Shifting in the saddle, he could just make out the cabins on the lakeshore far below. Pale gray tendrils curled from the stone chimney atop his. Winona was up early, making breakfast for Evelyn and her.

Presently, the sun cleared the horizon. High above, the glacier gleamed bright, brighter than the ivory snow that mantled adjacent peaks, the brightest splash of white in all that vast vista of green and brown.

Nate wondered why To-Ma had sought refuge there, of all places. Was it because no one would bother him? Or had the boy been drawn by the shiny ice and decided to stay?

Neota coughed to get his attention, and when Nate looked around, he signed, "We hear no shoot last night."

"I know," Nate signed. The Ute was suggesting that was a good omen. That if To-Ma was trying to harm Zach and Louisa, surely there would be gunfire. But Nate did not share Neota's optimism. He had too much experience under his wide leather belt. He knew all too chillingly well how swiftly, and silently, death could strike. It might be that they had not heard gunfire because Zach and Lou were not alive to squeeze the trigger.

As if to prove Nate wrong, a vagrant gust of wind from on high bore with it a faint but unmistakable sound, one that sent fear coursing through Nate's big frame. It was the one sound he hoped not to hear, a sound that told him more than any other possibly could.

It was a scream. The scream of a woman in terror for her life, or for the life of another, or both.

Chapter Sixteen

The Thing, as Zach and Lou had come to think of their relentless pursuer, climbed slowly toward them, a growl rumbling in its barrel chest.

It was close enough that Zach could see its eyes glitter with star shine. They were fixed as intently on him as the eyes of a stalking bear or cougar. He aimed between them. All it would take was a stroke of the trigger, and he could end their harrowing ordeal.

"Shoot!" Lou whispered. Zach was waiting too long, she thought. He wanted to be sure, but the Thing was too close. If by some chance he missed or the shot was not mortal, the Thing would be on them before Zach could reload.

Zach held his breath and steadied his arms. The moment had come. The Thing was no more then ten feet below them. He was so confident, he smiled as he tightened his finger. There was a flash, but not the crashing boom that should follow. *A misfire.* Instantly Zach reached for the ramrod but the harm had been done.

With a roar that did not seem like it could come from a human throat, the Thing launched itself at them, hurtling up the trunk with astounding speed. That something so huge could move so quick was not unusual; buffalo were remarkably agile despite their size, and bears were fast when they wanted to be. But the Thing was faster than both, faster than anything Zach ever went up against. It was on him in a heartbeat.

Instinctively, Zach jabbed the Hawken at its glittering eyes, seeking to slow it down. But a giant hand sheathed in a bear paw closed around the barrel and wrenched the Hawken from his grasp. Zach tried to hold on, but the Thing's strength was as immense as its size. The Hawken went clattering toward the earth, bouncing off branch after branch.

The Thing howled, swiped its claws at Zach's legs. Jerking them aside, Zach grabbed for his bowie. Honed razor sharp, it could open man or beast with a single slash. He almost had it clear of the beaded sheath when thunder clapped in his ear and a cloud of acrid smoke enveloped him. For a few anxious seconds all he saw was the smoke. Coughing, he swiped at the cloud, then looked down in consternation. "Where—" he began.

The Thing was gone.

"It dropped when I shot it," Lou said excitedly. "I think I killed it."

Zach was not so sure. A body that huge would

make a lot of noise falling and there had been no sound at all, which told him the Thing had descended under its own power. "I lost the Hawken."

"I know. I saw it drop." Louisa shoved the other pistol at him, then started reloading the one she had fired. "Keep your eyes peeled, just in case."

Zach did not need the urging. Holding on to a limb, he swung out from the trunk to peer behind it. He scoured the lower limbs for movement but saw none.

"If it isn't dead it has to be hurt," Lou said as she opened her ammo pouch. "I couldn't have missed."

"If it's alive, it will try again," Zach said. He sat and held the flintlock in his lap. If not for Lou, the Thing would have done to him as it had done to the Hawken and he would be lying on the damp earth, broken and bleeding. "Thank you, by the way."

Lou's grin was white against the black. "I've sort of gotten used to you keeping my bed warm at night."

Zach's answering grin died as a fierce snarl confirmed his hunch. He glanced down. The Thing was circling the tree, and it was in a foul temper. Snarls and roars and growls tore at the fabric of the night.

"I thought for sure I shot it in the head." Lou did not mask her disappointment.

"Maybe you did," Zach said. Head shots were not always fatal. Some animals, notably bear and buffalo had such thick skulls, slugs did not always penetrate. And the bear skin would also help protect their attacker.

"Just so it stays down there and leaves us be," Lou said. Dawn would break eventually. All they had to do was hold out until the sun drove the Thing into hiding.

Zach was of the same mind. He was content to stay in the tree all night if they had to.

Time crawled. The roars and growls went on and on. When, abruptly, they stopped, both Zach and Lou leaned out, their ears cocked, expecting the bestial din to resume. But the night stayed quiet except for the shriek of wind from off the cold slopes at the summit.

"What is it up to?" Zach wondered.

"Maybe it left."

Zach did not believe that for a moment. So long as breath remained in that giant body, the Thing would not give up. "Make yourself as comfortable as you can," he said. "It's going to be a long night."

Lou leaned back. But comfort was out of the question. The limb she was straddling was scarcely thick enough to support her weight. The slightest lapse in her concentration, and she would slip.

"Hold these for me," Zach said, extending the pistol and the bowie.

"What are you doing?" Lou asked, but instead of answering, he unbuckled his leather belt and held it out to her. "What am I supposed to do with this?"

"Take off your belt and hook them together. They should be long enough to wrap around the tree and you, both."

"Oh. So I won't fall. But what about you?"

"One of us can keep watch while the other rests," Zach proposed. "Since you didn't get any sleep last night, you go first."

"You didn't get much yourself," Lou said, remembering what he had told her before. But she didn't argue. She *was* ungodly tired. She handed back the pistol and the bowie, then had him hold her weapons while she removed her belt and hooked hers to his. Reaching around on either side of the trunk, she looped the belt around it, then shifted and sat with her back to the bole and secured the belt around her middle.

Zach smiled and touched her leg. "I know it will be hard but try to get some rest."

It was not hard at all. Lou closed her eyes and folded her arms, and just like that she was out.

"Louisa?" Zach said. When she did not reply, he rose close to her and noted the gentle rise and fall of her bosom. "I'll be damned," he said softly. Sinking back down, he hefted the pistol and the bowie. All of a sudden they seemed puny.

A gust caused the tree to sway. The wind was picking up. Zach did not think much of it since the wind usually picked up at night. But soon the gusts were coming one after the other, and growing stronger. It was a harbinger of a change in the weather.

That was all they needed, Zach reflected. A rainstorm or, worse, snow. That high up, snow fell even in the summer. And it was growing colder. The temperature had fallen five degrees in the past hour, unless he missed his guess. By morning they would be freezing.

Zach leaned back. The cold bit into his bones, sending a shiver rippling through him. But it also helped keep him awake. He moved his left leg to relieve a cramp, then gazed lovingly at his wife. So much for starting their family. If they had to go to this much trouble to make a baby, maybe they should get a dog. He grinned at the thought. But the truth was, deep down he wanted a child as much as she did. A son, to carry on the King line. A boy he could take hunting and fishing and instruct in the ways of a warrior. That would be grand.

The tree shook again, the wind knifing into him. He saw stars to the west blink out as if they had been devoured. A storm front was moving in, the clouds nigh invisible in the darkness. "Just what we need," he grumbled aloud. Nothing was going right. The next time Lou suggested they take a ride up into the high country, he was going to throw her in the lake.

The tree would not stop shaking. The keen of the wind rose and fell like the wail of an angry specter. Suddenly the wind died. In the lull the tree continued to shake.

It shouldn't, but it did.

Zach sat up and looked down. Nothing was below him. He smiled, blaming frayed nerves. Then he felt the bole move yet again, and he whipped around and glanced down the other side of the spruce.

The Thing was almost to them.

Zach hollered for Lou to wake up even as he thrust his pistol at the Thing's face and thumbed back the hammer. He always thought he was quick, but compared to the monster in the bear hide he was molasses. An iron bear paw shot out and slammed Zach's arm against the trunk. Pain lanced clear up to Zach's shoulder and his arm went momentarily numb. The flintlock was torn away and sent arcing into the night sky.

The Thing launched itself at him. Zach heard Lou scream his name. Then fingers as hard as rock clamped on to his throat and others on to his buckskin shirt. He was ripped from his roost and swept over the Thing's head. Another moment, and the Thing would hurl him to the earth below. It would be a miracle if every bone in his body was not broken.

Desperate, Zach stabbed and slashed with the bowie. He scored, too, cutting the Thing's shoulders and arms and the neck once. The Thing roared and twisted and must have lost its footing because suddenly it was falling and taking Zach with it.

Zach tried to wrest free. The Thing was too strong. He slammed onto a limb and pain seared his ribs. He clutched at the branch but could not hold on. Again there was the sensation of falling, stopped by another branch. This time his head and shoulder bore the brunt, and the night exploded in a swirl of fireflies. He was dimly aware of continuing to fall, of another jarring blow. Then came the hardest jolt of all and the fireflies faded to black.

Fingers were plucking at him. Warm drops were falling on his face. Zach opened his eyes, and never had Louisa looked so lovely. Her own eyes were moist.

"Can you hear me? Where are you hurt?"

"All over," Zach said, and grinned. He could still feel the iron fingers on his throat even though they were not there. He tried to rise. "The Thing! Where did it get to?"

"I don't know." Lou looked right and left. "There was no sign of it when I climbed down." Fear had lent her wings. Fear that when she reached the bottom she would find the man she loved dead.

Zach rose on his elbows. "It has to be near."

"Maybe you hurt it with your knife or it was hurt when it fell," Lou said. But it would not give up. Not that monster.

Zach stared at his empty hands. "My bowie. I must have dropped it. Do you see it anywhere?"

"No," Lou said. As dark as it was, finding it could take forever. "I still have mine." Drawing her knife, she pressed the hilt into his palm.

"One knife and one pistol," Zach said. He did not need to elaborate. Grimacing, he sat up. He had either cracked a few ribs or come awful close. Just taking a deep breath hurt.

"You shouldn't move," Lou said.

"We need to hunt for cover." Zach ignored the pain and stood. He took her hand and made toward what he took to be a cluster of boulders. But he had only taken a couple of steps when his left leg nearly gave out.

Lou slipped her arm around his waist to support him. "What's the matter?"

"My ankle," Zach said. It did not feel broken. He figured he had twisted it. Gingerly, he tried walking and was able to limp to the boulders. He eased down, then raised his pant leg. A cursory grope showed his ankle to be swollen. "Damn."

"I wonder where the Thing got to."

The sky had clouded over. The night was nearly pitch-black. There were hours to go until daylight, too, a fact Zach tried not to dwell on. "Sit down," he said, and patted the ground next to him.

"But the Thing," Lou said.

"Knows right where we are. But with our backs to this boulder, it can only get at us from the front."

Lou did not like the idea, but she did as he asked. Holding the pistol in both hands, she drew back the hammer. "Why hasn't it jumped us yet?"

"Who knows?" Zach rejoined. He was just glad it hadn't. He had no illusions about the outcome, not when all he had was a knife and with his ankle swollen like it was.

"We need your rifle and the other pistol," Lou said. With them they stood a chance of holding the creature off.

"They could be anywhere," Zach said.

"I doubt they fell far from the tree," Lou said. "I'll go look."

Zach grabbed her wrist as she started to stand. "You'll do no such thing. We stick together."

"Three guns are better than one," Lou persisted. The rifle most of all. She had seen her husband drop a bull buffalo at two hundred yards with it.

"I need to rest my ankle," Zach said, "and we are not separating." He was not letting her out of his sight.

A growl from out of the ink ended their argument. Lou raised her pistol, but had nothing to shoot. "Do you see it?"

Zach shook his head. He waited for the Thing to growl again and it did, but from a different spot. "It's moving," he warned. "Circling us."

Lou pushed onto a knee. "Stay behind me when it charges. I won't let it get you."

Most men would be pleased to have a wife who cared so much, she would sacrifice her life for his. But her words stung Zach to his core. He was the husband. He should be the one protecting her, not the other way around. Accordingly, gritting his teeth, he slowly stood. Lou had her back to him and did not notice.

"There!" she suddenly cried, and pointed.

Zach saw it, too. A large bearlike shape to their left. The pounding thud of heavy feet smote his ears a split second before he realized the Thing was charging. He hobbled past Lou, the knife in front of him.

"What do you think you are doing?"

Her question was never answered. For even as Zach set himself, the Thing was on him.

Louisa screamed.

Chapter Seventeen

Zach King slashed the knife out and up and felt it bite flesh. Then he was swept off his feet and flung into the air. The sky and the ground changed places. He crashed down hard. Dazed, he might have lain there indefinitely had Lou not cried out.

"Let go of me!"

Zach heaved off the ground and lurched to her aid. His ankle protested, but he forced his leg to move.

Lou was furiously battling the Thing. It had one arm around her waist and was trying to pin her arms with the other. Intent on her to the exclusion of all else, the Thing was unaware of Zach's approach.

Zach sank the hunting knife into the creature's back.

The howl that rose to the roiling clouds drowned out the wind. The Thing let go of Lou and spun. It towered over Zach, its features contorted in rage. Zach had yanked the knife out as the Thing turned, and now he thrust the bloody blade at its chest. By rights the point should have sheared the Thing's brutish heart. But Zach had forgotten how incredibly quick it was. His arm was seized and nearly wrenched from the socket. It was all Zach could do to hold on to the hilt. Another instant, and he was given a shove that sent him stumbling. His ankle a wellspring of raw pain, he started back toward them. But he was too late.

The Thing had scooped Lou into an arm and was bounding up the slope.

"No!" Zach gave chase, but he could not possibly hope to catch them, even if his ankle was not sprained.

Lou was beating at the monster's face and neck and kicking at its groin. The thick bear hide protected it, but she did clip its nose and hit his throat squarely. Yet her punches had no more effect than if she had swatted the Thing with paper. Then she saw an eye fixed on her in anger and she reacted without any thought for the consequences; she raked her nails across the eyeball.

The Thing's cry of torment was the loudest yet. It threw Lou down and covered its stricken eye with a huge hand.

Lou came up in a crouch. She had no intention of fighting it, and she whirled to race to Zach. Before she could take a step, a tree-trunk leg slammed into her chest, flipping her like a coin. She struck a tree and collapsed. On the verge of passing out, she saw her husband, limping badly, almost to the creature. "Zach! No!"

A red haze had fallen over Zach's eyes. Rage boiled in him like scalding water. Over and over in his brain pounded the same thought: The Thing had hurt Lou, the Thing had hurt Lou, the Thing had hurt Lou.

The Thing was hunched over and still had a hand over its eye. Blood trickled between its fingers and down its cheek. It must have heard or sensed Zach, because suddenly it turned.

Zach thrust the hunting knife into the Thing's chest. Again he went for the heart. But all the man-beast did was glance down, grunt, and unleash an open-handed blow that nearly knocked Zach loose of his moccasins.

Flat on his back, the world spinning, Zach saw the creature loom over him. He tried to rise to defend himself, but his body would not cooperate. A bear-paw hand reached for his throat, and the Thing bared its teeth in anticipation. Wet drops spattered Zach's face. He thought for a second they were drops of blood from the wounds he had inflicted.

More drops fell, cold drops in a driving rain.

The Thing paused. It tilted its great head back and gaped skyward in fascination, as a small child might do.

Zach scrambled away. Arms and legs churning, he scuttled until he came up against a boulder. By then the rain was descending in driving sheets. He could not see the Thing. Nor could the Thing see him. A roar warned him the abomination had discovered its quarry was no longer at its feet.

Zach had lost his hold on the knife. He was unarmed and virtually defenseless. He groped wildly about for a jagged rock or a branch or anything else he could use as a weapon.

The cascading torrent was making so much noise, Zach did not hear the Thing come toward him. He saw it, though, when it hove out of the deluge. Why the Thing did not see him, he would never know. But it sloshed on past, a gigantic lumbering waterfall.

Zach stiffly rose. He moved toward where he had last seen Lou, or where he *thought* he had see her. It was impossible to tell in the downpour. Everything was a wet blur, even his own hand at arm's length. His sense of direction was skewed; he could not even tell north from south or east from west. He had to rely on instinct.

Zach went as far as thought he should have to go but did not find her. He searched in small circles, then larger ones. Fear chewed at his vitals. Maybe the Thing had found her first and was carrying her off, back up to its lair in the glacier.

Which direction was up? Zach wondered. The rain was so heavy, he couldn't say. He walked faster, heedless of his fear. He searched and searched. Repeatedly he bumped into trees and boulders or became entangled in brush. For hours he hunted, his despair mounting until he was nearly beside himself.

Eventually fatigue and his ankle would not be denied. Zach sank to his knees with his forehead on the ground, closed his eyes, and did something he had not done since he became a man; he cried. He could not stop the tears if he tried, and he did not try. More fully than ever, he realized how much Louisa meant to him. He had never loved anyone as much as he loved her. No, not even his parents or his sister, and he loved them dearly.

Zach quietly shed tears until there were no tears left to shed. He did not get back up. He stayed there, eyes shut, soaked to the skin, his ankle throbbing, his bruises hurting, and waited for the rain to end or dawn to break, whichever came first.

As it turned out, both occurred about the same time.

He was conscious of the rain slackening and the wind dying. He raised his head and opened his eyes and beheld a brighter world than when he had shut them. The rain ended just as a golden crescent promised a rebirth of the sun. The clouds were breaking up. The storm had gone on down the mountain and was drenching the valley floor and the comfortable cabin they had forsaken for their romantic frolic.

Zach snorted. From now on he would confine his romancing to their bedroom. They would live longer that way.

The notion sobered him. Zach rose and tested his ankle. It ached but not quite as severely. He was facing east and turned to the northwest, in the direction of the glacier. Astonishment rooted him in place, but only until his heart swelled near to bursting. "Lou!" he cried, and ran limping toward her with his arms spread wide.

* * *

Lou had spent a god-awful night, soaked and miserable and worried sick about Zach. She had tried to find him. Hour after hour she hunted, always in dread of encountering the Thing. But she came across neither of them, and about an hour before sunrise she curled up under the overspreading boughs of an evergreen. She did not think she could sleep, given her emotional state, but she surprised herself.

Now the rain had ended and the sun was rising, and Lou stepped out from under the tree. She was terribly cold and as hungry as could be, but neither compared to the ache in her heart. She was afraid the Thing had killed the man who meant more to her than life itself. "Oh, Zach," she whispered forlornly. "What will I do without you?"

Then Lou heard her name and looked up in disbelief and joy. She flew to him, flew into his arms and hugged him to her and kissed his cheeks and his chin and his forehead and uttered endearments that in public would make her blush. They clung to one another in the ferocity of their love, the world around them forgotten.

Suddenly Zach scooped her into his arms and carried her under the tree. "We will rest awhile and dry out some."

But they did not rest, and what little drying they did went unnoticed.

It was the middle of the morning when Zach roused and sat up. The forest had a fresh vitality about it, courtesy of the storm. Everything looked shiny and new. He gently shook Lou. "We should be on our way."

With the sun up much of their confidence was restored. The Thing hated the daylight. It always sought cover. They had ten hours to put as many miles behind them as they could. With luck they would cover so much ground, the Thing would never find them.

They hiked along hand in hand, smiling, happy, until a loud grunt from out of a stand of aspens reminded them they were weaponless. They hunkered, thinking a grizzly had caught their scent, and they had gone from the proverbial frying pan into the fire. But it was a small black bear that shambled into view. It had no inkling they were there and went off to the north grumbling to itself in typical bear fashion.

"Bears and men have a lot in common," Lou whispered as they moved on.

"So do women and shrews."

Lou poked him with an elbow, and smiled. "Tease me all you want. Nothing can spoil my mood today."

But she was wrong. Something could spoil it, and did, when an unearthly howl rent the clear, bright air, causing birds to take nervous wing and sending deer into panicked flight. They turned and raked the woodland but saw only vegetation.

"It's close," Lou whispered.

"Too close." Zach looked around, spotted a fist-sized rock with a sawtooth edge, and snatched it up.

"But this can't be," Lou said. "The light hurts its eyes."

"Maybe it wants you bad enough, it doesn't care." Zach clasped her hand and backed down the mountain until he was sure they were not being pursued. Then he broke into an awkward jog, awkward because he could not put his full weight on his sprained ankle.

"What do we do if it catches up to us?"

"Need you ask? We kill the son of a bitch."

"With a rock?"

She had a point, Zach mused. They needed something better. A spear would be nice, but without a knife he could not sharpen a suitable limb. A club would serve better than the rock, but he did not put much faith in being able to stop the Thing with one. Still, he cast about until he found a downed branch that was thick enough. He trimmed it using the sawtooth rock and broke off one end. A few trial swings against a pine convinced him the club would not shatter when he needed it most.

Lou took the sawtooth rock. "I almost blinded it once. With this I can do a better job."

Zach hoped to God the Thing did not get its hands on her again. He would do anything to prevent that. Even to losing his life to save hers.

They hiked on, the shadows of the tall trees alternating with bright patches of sunlight. Here and there sunbeams shimmered like pillars of ethereal flax. The forest in all its pristine glory stretched before them.

"Notice something?" Lou asked.

"How cute your button nose is?"

"No. Notice how quiet it is. On a day like this the birds should be singing and squirrels should be making a racket. But there is nothing. No sounds at all."

Zach had in fact noticed, but he had not said anything to avoid worrying her more than she already was. He shrugged. "It could be anything."

"Don't lie to me, Zachary King," Louisa scolded. "It's one thing and one thing only. *The* Thing. That hideous beast who has been tormenting us. He must be near."

"Not in the daytime, remember?" Zach said. "He's holed up somewhere. He won't be after us until dark." Zach did not feel as confidant as he tried to sound. The Thing shunned daylight, yes, but that did not necessarily mean it could not be abroad if it wanted to be. He looked at the club in his hand. He would gladly trade it for a pistol or a knife.

"I hope you're right," Lou said.

The minutes became hours.

Their spirits were determined, but their bodies were tired and battered, and by one in the afternoon they were both dragging.

"We should rest," Lou proposed.

Zach did not want to stop. Distance equated to safety. He had been pushing to cover a lot of ground so he could spare Lou yet more terror.

"Please," Louisa said when he did not respond. "I'm wore out. If we don't stop I'll keel over before too long."

"Very well," Zach said. A tiny voice deep inside prodded him to keep going, but he halted and stood watching their back trail as she wearily sank down with her back to a tree.

"I'm thirsty enough to drink the lake," Lou commented.

During the violence of the night they had

drifted from the vicinity of the stream. Zach figured it was north of them and offered to go find it.

"Not alone, you don't," Lou said. "We stay together from here on out."

Zach had no objection. She stood and they moved quietly through the greenery, expecting at any moment to hear the familiar gurgle.

"Where is it?" Lou wondered. "We can't have strayed that far."

It was obvious they had. In the heavy rain and the dark and confusion they had drifted a considerable way. Zach squinted at the sun, and stopped. "Can you hold out until evening?" A day without water would not kill her, but he did not say that out loud. Some remarks a husband should keep to himself.

"If I have to." Lou had endured worse.

Zach held her hand and they bent their steps down a succession of thickly wooded and not so wooded slopes. By the sun it was pushing four o'clock when they crossed a grassy bench and came to a slope covered with rank after rank of shadowed firs.

"Not more of those," Zach said.

"It's dark in there," Lou remarked. She glanced at the sun to reassure herself they had hours yet before it set.

"We can go around," Zach suggested. He did not like the firs, either. They grew too close together.

"And waste a lot of time we can't afford to waste," Lou said. "Maybe it's best if we push on."

Zach nodded. Their shoulders touching, they moved along a narrow aisle between lodgepoles. A preternatural gloom pervaded the stillness. Not so much as a chirp or a flutter of wings. Even the breeze did not penetrate. There was just the two of them and the trees and the shadows.

"Maybe we should have gone around," Lou said.

Zach did not remember passing through this particular belt of firs on the ride up. He was hoping they would come to the end soon, but the firs went on and on and on.

"When we get home," Lou said, "the first thing I'm going to do is heat water and fill the washbasin to the brim. A hot bath would do wonders."

Zach never cared for hot baths, himself. He preferred a morning dip in the cold, clear lake.

"Then I will put on clean buckskins and cook a meal fit for a regiment. So much food, we'll explode if we eat it all."

"Eggs for me," Zach said, his mouth watering at the delicious prospect. "Ten or twelve, scrambled."

Lou warmed to the subject. It took her mind off what might be out there. "I should think you would want a thick, juicy slab of venison. I know I do. With potatoes and peas from the garden. And a slice or two of bread smothered in that butter your mother makes. For dessert we can have pie and pudding, both. How does that sound?"

"It sounds as if in five years I'll be calling you fatty."

Louisa laughed, the first time she had done so since she had been abducted. She turned to hug him, the laugh dying in her throat when a crepitant growl seemed to issue from all directions at once.

Zach whirled and raised his club. The growl died before he could tell where it came from.

"It could be a bear or a mountain lion," Lou

whispered. Her rock suddenly seemed less than useless.

"You know better." Zach motioned, and ran as fast as he could. Lou matched him step for step. Ordinarily he was far swifter, but his ankle would not let him go full speed.

"I don't see it anywhere."

Neither did Zach. But it was shadowing them. He was sure. He stared ahead, looking for the end of the firs. Their best hope lay in reaching a meadow or some other open space.

"There!" Lou shouted, and pointed.

A gargantuan shape had flitted between firs to their right. One instant it was there and the next it was gone. But there was no mistaking what it was. Bears did not lope on two legs.

"We can't run forever." Lou was puffing and had a pain in her side. Her feet were lead weights.

"I'll carry you if I have to," Zach said, forgetting, for the moment, his ankle.

Lou saved her breath for running. She had never been so tired. She had to force her legs to move. She thought of Winona and Nate, and how sad they would be if anything happened to their son, and she regretted bringing Zach so far to do what they could have done in the security of their cabin.

Zach was concentrating on the firs to the right. He figured if the Thing charged them, that was the direction it would come from. But once more he had not reckoned on its uncanny speed. A cry from Lou warned him.

The Thing was in front of them. It stood between two firs, barring their way, an enormous mass of bear hide and menace, its huge hands opening and closing. Incredibly, the hilt of the hunting knife still stuck from its chest.

"Dear God," Lou breathed.

Zach stepped in front of her. "I'll keep it busy. When I say to, I want you to run and not look back."

"I will not abandon you."

Not taking his eyes off the man-beast, Zach said, "Don't argue. It's the only chance you have." At that, it was a slim one.

"What about you? You can't hold it off alone." Lou moved up next to him. "I'm staying, and that's that."

Again Zach stepped in front of her. "Go, damn it."

"Stop your cussing. Your father never swears and Shakespeare hardly ever, and you do it entirely too much."

Zach was flabbergasted. He could not comprehend how she could nitpick about his swearing when their lives were at stake.

"As for leaving, I took you for better or for worse and it can't get much worse than this." Lou moved up next to him again.

This whole while, the Thing had stood there staring. Now it roared and attacked.

Zach ducked under its outflung arms and swung his club. He caught the Thing in the knee and its legs buckled. Whipping the club overhead, he was on the verge of bashing its head in when a powerful backhand caught him across the chest and he was hurled against a fir.

Lou leaped in. She swung the sawtooth rock at

the Thing's eyes, but it had learned its lesson and got an arm up to protect its face. She pivoted, thinking to dart in under its arm and slash it across the throat. A cuff to her temple thwarted her and left her stretched out on her back with her head pealing like a struck gong.

"Lou!" Zach sprang and swung at the Thing's other knee. The *crack* was as loud as a pistol shot. The Thing staggered. Zach swung in a frenzy, hitting its arm, its chest, a shoulder, everywhere but where he wanted to hit it, which was on the head.

The Thing was slow to react. It was gazing at Lou. Zach had landed half a dozen blows before the Thing tore its eyes from her and looked at him. Zach swung yet again, but the Thing seized the club and sought to wrest it from his grasp.

Zach clung on. "Run, Lou!" he yelled. A huge hand slammed into his shoulder and he wound up on his face in the dirt. He rolled, not a moment too soon; a giant foot stomped down exactly where his head had been.

Lou was on her feet. She leaped at the Thing to buy Zach time to get to his. She slashed the sawtooth rock across the Thing's arm but only cut the bear hide. A hand closed on her throat, and suddenly she was dangling in the air with the life slowly being choked out of her.

Zach voiced a Shoshone war whoop and swung the club with all his might. A huge hand swooped to his throat, and then he, too, was dangling in the air and fingers like metal spikes began to crush his neck. He could not breathe. He beat at the arm that held him, but it was like beating a log. Zach glanced at Lou and she glanced at him and their eyes locked. They said with their eyes what they could not say with their mouths: *I love you.*

Both heard a *twang.* Both saw the Thing arch its back, then swivel its great misshapen head. A roar shook the firs. The Thing let go of them, and turned.

Zach fell to his knees. As if in a dream state he saw an arrow embedded in the Thing's broad back. Beyond, another arrow nocked to the string of his bow, stood a Ute warrior Zach recognized: Neota. Next to Neota was Zach's father, a rifle to his shoulder.

As the Thing lurched into motion Neota loosed the shaft. He let another fly when it was halfway to them, one more as it reared to strike. For a few seconds the Thing was motionless. Then it slowly oozed to earth as choking sounds came from its throat and blood from its mouth and nostrils.

Neota knelt and placed his hand on the Thing's shoulder. He said something in the Ute language and bowed his head.

Nate ran to Zach and Lou and helped them to sit up. "Are you all right?"

All both could do was nod.

"It's over," Nate told them. "You're safe."

Coughing and sputtering to clear his throat, Zach managed to say, "Thank you, Pa."

Louisa rubbed her throat and sucked in a deep breath. "You can't imagine what it was like. You saved us from a horrible monster."

Nate gazed at the still form in the bear hide and

at the living portrait in sorrow. "He saved you, not me." Nate paused. They deserved to know the full story. Or did they? On second thought, maybe he should let them go on thinking it was a monster. They would sleep better at night.

A lot better than Neota.

BLOOD TRAIL TO KANSAS

ROBERT J. RANDISI

Ted Shea thinks he is a goner for sure. All the years he's worked to build his Montana spread and fine herd of prime beef means nothing if he can't sell them. And with a vicious rustler and his gang of cutthroats scaring all the hands, no one is willing to take to the trail. Until Dan Parmalee drifts into town. A gunman and gambler with a taste for long odds, he isn't about to let a little hot lead part him from some cold cash. But it doesn't take Dan long to realize this isn't just any run. This is a...*Blood Trail to Kansas*.

ISBN 10: 0-8439-5799-9
ISBN 13: 978-0-8439-5799-0 $5.99 US/$7.99 CAN

THE LAST WAY STATION
KENT CONWELL

As soon as Jack Slade and his partner, Three Fingers Bent, arrive in the small Texas town of New Gideon, they know no one wants them there. There's been some rustling in the area, and folks aren't taking too kindly to strangers. But things don't get any better when Slade and Bent move on. The two don't get far before a posse from New Gideon rides up, accuses Bent of murder, and takes him back to face a judge. Slade knows he won't have much time before his partner hangs on a trumped-up charge, and there's only one way he can save his friend—he'll have to find the real killer himself!

ISBN 10: 0-8439-5928-2
ISBN 13: 978-0-8439-5928-4 $5.99 US/$7.99 CAN

To order a book or to request a catalog call:
1-800-481-9191
This book is also available at your local bookstore, or you can check out our Web site **www.dorchesterpub.com** where you can look up your favorite authors, read excerpts, or glance at our discussion forum to see what people have to say about your favorite books.

RIDERS OF PARADISE

ROBERT J. HORTON

Clint and Dick French may be identical twins, but Clint's wild ways contrast sharply with his brother's more sophisticated tastes. But then Dick decides to share his brother's responsibilities at the family ranch—and ends up sharing his enemies as well. When notorious troublemaker Blunt Rodgers mistakes Dick for Clint, the tenderfoot looks to be doomed. Three shots are fired, Blunt ends up dead, and the sheriff doesn't need evidence to peg Clint the killer. And once word gets back to the infamous outlaw Blunt rode with, a whole gang of hardcases will be gunning for *both* brothers.

ISBN 10: 0-8439-5895-2
ISBN 13: 978-0-8439-5895-9 $5.99 US/$7.99 CAN

THE BLAZE OF NOON

TIM CHAMPLIN

The blistering road through Arizona Territory is called the Devil's Highway for a good reason. And now Dan Mora knows why. He's met all kinds of challenges on the trail, and he'll be in big trouble if he doesn't soon find water. Hugh Deraux knows the same stifling thirst. Breaking out of prison was easy compared to this trek through the unforgiving desert. But both men are driven by more than thirst. They hunger for the riches rumored to be found along the dangerous trail. And nothing will stop them from claiming the treasure—not each other, not Apaches, not even...*The Blaze of Noon*.

ISBN 10: 0-8439-5892-8
ISBN 13: 978-0-8439-5892-8 $5.99 US/$7.99 CAN

#50
WILDERNESS

PEOPLE OF THE FOREST

SPECIAL GIANT EDITION!

David Thompson

When Nate King chose a new valley in which to build his home, he wanted to get away from all civilization and the inevitable trouble it brings. But Nate can't duck trouble for very long. A hostile band of Indians has also laid claim to the Kings' valley, and they've made it clear they're not willing to share. In a desperate act to punish Nate and his family, they capture his daughter, Evelyn. And Nate will do anything it takes—even if it means sacrificing his own life—to get her back.

#51
WILDERNESS

COMANCHE MOON

David Thompson

In the untamed wilderness of the majestic Rockies, Nate King has often seen that the line between life and death is a thin one. So far he's managed to stay on the right side, but all that could change on a rare excursion to Bent's Fort. While there, he finds a greenhorn couple looking to settle in the heart of Comanche territory. Unable to leave them helpless, Nate puts himself right in the middle of the warpath. But when an old enemy steals all his supplies and weapons, Nate's left utterly defenseless against a band of vicious warriors who want nothing more than to see him dead.

BAD MAN'S GULCH

One sheriff and two deputies have already disappeared in the rough-and-tumble mining town of Slosson's Gulch. The same fate awaits any other man who crosses the cut-throats and thieves who thrive there. Pedro Melendez is a gambler and a drifter, trying his best to put his gunslinging days behind him. But he'll need all the sharpshooting he can muster to help a vulnerable young woman find her missing father—because there are plenty of miners eager to make sure Pedro is the next one to go missing.